SKY COMMAND

SKY
COMMAND

by

ANTON RICHLER

*

A TROJAN PAPERBACK

Published by Trojan Publications – London

All characters in this book are fictional and any resemblance to persons living or dead is purely coincidental

Printed in Great Britain by
Hunt Barnard Printing Ltd.

CHAPTER I

The Tide of Fortune

For two whole days, the wind had blown steadily out of the north-east. A cold wind, rising to gale force, bringing the heavily-laden snow-clouds in its wake, sweeping over the smooth, barren stretch of the airfield, howling thinly in the telegraph wires that bordered the perimeter track. The previous night, the enemy had failed to put in an appearance; either the bombers of the R.A.F. had attacked targets far to the south, or had not put in any operational flight over the country at all.

But this time, it might be different. The mercury in the barometer crept down slowly and outside, beyond the frosted windows, the snow was just beginning to fall. Whenever the door of the Operations Room was opened, the one door which led directly outside connecting us with the arctic world, the air would swirl into the room, filled with tiny, cutting knives that froze our bodies to the marrow, chilled our faces and numbed our hands and feet.

For perhaps three minutes there had been silence, complete, utter silence in the room. The high, whistling whine of the wind seemed unnaturally loud. It made me feel vaguely uncomfortable.

Slowly, quite deliberately, Graeber, the Commandant, crushed out his cigarette in the metal tray, held the butt in his fingers for a long moment, staring down at it almost bitterly. Then, with a gesture which held a curious air of finality and decision, he got to his feet, scraping back the chair, his hand stretching out for the gloves lying on the table in front of him.

"Every pilot will be ready for immediate take-off," he said curtly. There was a deep and intense weariness in his voice and the strain showed on his face, shadowed by the pale light from the single blue bulb set close against the whitewashed ceiling.

"Oh God, sir, no. Not tonight again!" moaned Jensen, one of the older pilots, a battle-scarred man who had survived more than five dozen dog-fights in the air over Germany and earlier, far back at the beginning of the war, even as far afield as the coasts of Britain when the Luftwaffe had been a tremendous fighting force, bombing the enemy cities almost unhampered.

"*Ja*, tonight again, I'm afraid." Graeber snapped the words harshly. He regarded the other moodily. "There are times," he went on tiredly, "when I could almost love the British. Their unfailing promptness and regularity makes them almost unique."

"And you think they will come tonight, sir?" I straightened and leaned forward in my chair. "The weather must have kept them grounded last night—and tonight the wind is, if anything, even stronger. Visibility will be bad at five thousand feet."

"Could be," the Commandant agreed. He nodded sardonically. "But that won't prevent them from coming." His voice dropped to a murmur. "They intend to destroy us, hammer us into submission. Already, they've reduced our armament production by close on sixty per cent. If it continues this way, we'll be forced to sue for peace whether the Fuhrer likes it or not."

He paused for a few seconds, his eyes speculative, then looked back at Jensen. "I know how you feel. I know how every man under my command feels at this very moment. I haven't been up there, but I have lost just as much sleep as the rest of you and my job hasn't been easy, trying to fight an air war with less than half the machines needed and operating with a handful of pilots, almost all of them on the verge of collapse. You can bet that the British Intelligence have a shrewd idea of our position. They know the whereabouts of every airfield still in commission, roughly how many planes are still serviceable, how low our petrol supplies are. everything.

"Kassel has been bombed several nights in succession with the single exception of last night. It seems unlikely that they will give us any respite. It's a strategic target and we are one of the few airfields still open within range of the city."

Jensen looked at him. His face was expressionless. Outside, there was the sound of heavy, hurried footsteps on the concrete, oddly muffled, and I guessed that already, the snow was beginning to settle. The wind was almost gale force. It would be virtually impossible to get into the air, and equally difficult to stay there for any length of time. In such a small plane as a Messerschmitt or a Heinkel, there would be little chance of flying to a course plotted beforehand.

"You're still not convinced of what I've said, gentlemen?" went on the Commandant softly He tossed his gloves from hand to hand. "You find it hard to believe that the British bombers will come over again tonight, even with the weather as it is and the botttom dropping out of the barometer?" He savoured his words slowly, compressed his thin lips a trifle, looked around the Operations Room again.

"No, it doesn't sound too likely, does it? You would prefer to believe that they will remain grounded again?" He shook his head, bent forward a little in the faint light, smoothed out the gloves with his fingers. Then, walking swiftly, he crossed over to the desk, picked up the report forms clipped in a neat bundle, riffled through them carefully, reading aloud:

"Returned to base, 1745—two planes missing, believed shot down: Take off 1825, large force of enemy bombers heading towards Kassel, returned 0320—seven enemy bombers destroyed, three fighters missing." He flicked over the page, continuing in a dull monotone: "Further attack on Kassel by a force of R.A.F. bombers estimated at six hundred planes. Both flights took off at 1125, remained on the attack for two hours before returning to Base. No losses."

He looked up. "Need I go any further, gentlemen. I could continue, you know." He counted the pages. "Six nights in succession Kassel was bombed by the R.A.F. and we were forced to take off in defence of the city. Last night, for the first time in a week, they failed to arrive." He shook his head again, slowly, firmly. "That isn't any guarantee at all that we'll be equally lucky tonight. And don't look to this abominable weather to help you, it won't. Three nights ago, the temperature was well below freezing point. Engines wouldn't start, frozen solid. But still they came, through a blizzard."

His words, even his sharpened tone, the lashing sarcasm of his voice, failed to evoke any response from Jensen. Just as before, he sat motionless, seemingly unheeding in a vast indifference.

I saw the Commandant's face harden. He drew himself upright, hooked the sheaf of reports back onto the clip, then turned back. I saw the glint in his eyes and guessed at what was coming.

"I'm afraid you seem to have things a little distorted, gentlemen. I fully realise the strain which every one of you has been through, especially during the past six weeks, but I don't think I have to remind you, all of you senior pilots on this airfield, that in total war such as this, when Germany is fighting the overwhelming strength of an aggressor, personal sufferings and individual feelings count as nothing. Germany must come first in all things." He walked over to the door again, paused with his fingers around the handle. "The whole future of Germany is at stake now," his voice was oddly quiet and restrained, unlike his previous outburst, "and nobody can have selfish feelings. Meanwhile, every pilot will hold himself in readiness throughout the night for immediate take-off. We may have little warning and it is essential that we should strike at them before they reach the outskirts of Kassel."

"And you think we can do anything really constructive, to prevent them from attacking whenever and wherever they please, sir?"

I turned my head sharply, saw the angry look in Eberbach's eyes. I saw, too, the deepening red flush in the Commandant's cheeks and recognised the signs only too well.

"What was that, Eberbach?" The other's voice was quiet and toneless, perfectly under control.

"I asked whether our little effort did anything to stop them from going through with their bombing raids, sir?" repeated the other, regarding Graeber steadily, unflinchingly. "We've got to look at this situation perfectly logically and frankly, sir. I realise you did a lot of flying before the war and in heavy bombers during the raids on London and Coventry, but do you know what it's really like up there now, especially in this kind of weather? Do you, sir? Somehow, I don't think you do.

"A Messerschmitt 109 isn't like a heavy four-engined bomber in that arctic wind. There's no keeping on one predetermined course with a crosswind of a hundred kilometres an hour hurling you all over the black sky, a blizzard making it impossible to see more than twenty metres in any direction, and the engine threatening to freeze up at any minute.

"Do you know what it's like with ice lying thick on your wings, trying to draw you down out of the sky and the clouds coming in heavy and fast so that you're on top of the enemy before you know where you are and their guns are hammmering at you from all directions? That's what it's like for us up there, night after night, without proper rest, without sleep, with every nerve drawn tight into threads of agony through your body, stretched to breaking point, your brain so numbed, so weary, that it combines with the rest to push you over the edge of insanity.

"When the mind and body reach that point, sir, a man would give anything just for the chance to let go, to close his eyes and fall asleep. Maybe—" here he paused and looked round at the rest of us before continuing, "—maybe, that's what happened to several of the men we've lost during the past few weeks. Maybe the enemy bullets did nothing, maybe they just felt that they'd had enough and they fell asleep at the controls. There's a limit to what a man can take in the way of punishment of that kind. Perhaps some people would call it suicide—but I prefer to think of it as something inevitable, something brought about by the terrible weariness which never leaves us, but goes on and on and on; and the fact that no one gets a chance to relax, even during the daytime."

Quite suddenly, he stopped, stubbed out his cigarette with a nervous, jerky movement of his hand and looked down at the grey smear of ash on his fingers, a look of vague distaste on his thin features. His eyes seemed brighter than usual and he licked his lips slowly.

I felt an odd feeling of surprise that he had been allowed

to continue without interruption. There had been an intense feeling in the other's voice, but the words had been polite and respectful.

Graeber regarded him steadily for a long moment, then nodded slowly. Just for a moment, he looked tired and beaten. Then he straightened his shoulders, raised himself to his full height.

"I'm afraid I had no idea that feeling ran so high in my command," he said quietly. "And believe me, the fact that I have to keep on sending you up there, without pause, night after night, has very little to do with me. I have my orders as you have yours; and we all have to see that they are carried out to the letter.

"The tide of fortune has changed radically for Germany. In the beginning, we had complete numerical superiority over the R.A.F. We ought to have driven them from the skies. But somehow, that never happened. Don't ask me to apportion the blame for that, because I can't do it. Someone failed somewhere, but that's beside the point. The pendulum has swung the other way. Now, we are in the position they were in, five years ago. But if they could do it, then I see no reason why we shouldn't."

Eberbach remained silent for a moment at the quietly spoken rebuke, then nodded his head slowly. "I'm sorry for that outburst, sir," he said slowly, "I suppose I was carried away for the moment. Things have been pretty tough during the past few nights and—" He broke off lamely and spread his hands in a futile, defensive gesture.

"I know, I know." Graeber looked at him, his face expressionless. "We're all talking out of turn. Every one of us is at the end of his endurance, but there's no alternative but to go on." His eyes rested on us with a long, speculative glance. Then he turned abruptly on his heel, opened the door and stepped out.

The frosty wind cut momentarily into us as an icy blast swirled around the room. Graeber struggled with the door for a moment, dragging it shut with all his strength, fighting against the inhuman force of the wind.

Shivering, I pulled myself to my feet, lit a cigarette and stared around at the others, elbows on their knees. Weariness was manifest in their attitudes, the utter, body-dragging weariness that could come only after days of exhaustion, nights with little or no sleep, the demand for concentration while engaging the enemy in that black, arctic world several thousand feet above the airfield.

"What does he think we are—machines?" ground out Hausser viciously. He lifted his head, peered at me in the dim light.

"Maybe he's right," said Jensen briefly. "We're on the receiving end now and there's nothing we can do about it. The R.A.F. know exactly where our factories are. They can bomb them whenever they like; their precision bombing is uncanny. No wonder we can do nothing against them. We need a breathing space to build up our strength again. How can we be expected to fight them with less than half the machines we need and our pilots being killed every night because they can't be relieved. This drain on men and machines will have to be halted before we can hope to meet the enemy on equal terms in the air."

I shook my head slowly. "There's no hope of that. Daily they become stronger while we—"

The shrill whine of the alarm killed the rest of my sentence. Instinctively, my eyes swung to the window beyond which lay only darkness and the faintly seen, drifting flakes of snow, thrown at intervals across my line of vision. At the corner of my eye, I saw Hausser running forward, snapping the blackout shutters into place and wondered vaguely how we could have overlooked this simple, but important precaution.

There had been little need for the shutters. With that shrill wind blowing the snow in a raging blizzard across the airfield, any ray of light which penetrated the darkness, could reach less than a few yards before being blotted out. Then we were all on our feet, tensed and expectant; the nerve-tingling wail of the alarm ringing in our ears.

It was, in a strangely undefinable way, a moment of decision as far as all of us were concerned. It was the moment when, if there were still any mutinous thoughts in the minds of the others, that these would come surging to the top of their thoughts, obliterating everything else; loyalty, courage, the ability to continue in spite of everything.

But the moment passed. Perhaps the reason was that even battle-weary minds still possessed some modicum of self-respect. Perhaps it was self-preservation. Whatever it was, we were all outside within seconds, the bitter wind cutting through our uniforms, catching our breath and tearing it from our lips so that our lungs remained starved as we ran forward, across the icy perimeter track, the snow beating into our eyes. It was impossible to see more than a dozen yards. Beyond that, there was nothing but a swirling, wind-driven curtain of white which blotted out all details.

The waiting fighters were out there, somewhere, my brain reasoned, even though I could see nothing of them.

The wailing alarm signal was silent now. Everything seemed hushed and deathly quiet, apart from the muffled pounding of our feet in the snow. Then there was a change in the texture of the ground under my feet, it became softer, more clinging, and I knew I was running on the grass of the airfield.

It was impossible to tell how far the enemy were away. The warning system was strained to its utmost limit in weather such as this and had been notoriously bad for the past two or three weeks. There was little reason why it should have been. The only planes flying over German soil nowadays were R.A.F. or American bombers, striking inland at our factories and rail junctions, bombing their targets almost unmolested.

Silence, a deep and complete silence around us, except for the soft thudding of boots on the ground and my own harsh breathing sounding oddly loud in my ears—and these sounds, oddly enough, only served to magnify the deep and clinging silence. Beside me, Hausser ran forward, his features occasionally visible in the faint glow thrown up off the ground by the thickening carpet of snow. His face, shockingly grey, strained and haggard, turned as though he felt my gaze on him.

"We're being thrown to the wolves, you know," he gasped, pushing the words out through his shaking lips. The wind plucked at them, tore them away even as he spoke, but I managed to catch them.

I nodded. Overhead, the clouds scudded against a leaden

sky, visible only when they appeared darker than the rest. My breath was gasping in my lungs by the time the dark shape of the plane loomed up directly ahead. I had run that road too many times during the past few days to have mistaken my direction. By now I could have done it blindfold, with an instinct which seemed quite natural.

The dark figures of the mechanics were just visible, huddling against the fuselage, striving to find a place to keep warm and out of the biting wind. They turned as I ran up to them.

"Everything's ready, sir."

I squinted through the driving snow, staring up at the other as he came forward, his collar pulled up against the wind.

"All fuelled up?"

The other grinned feebly at me. "She's been battered about, but I think she'll still hang together for a few more trips. Any idea how far they are away this time, sir?"

I shook my head. "No idea at all. Nobody seems to know anything these days. The whole system seems to have folded up completely. For all we know, they could be a hundred kilometres away and heading in a totally different direction. Maybe Kassel isn't their target this time."

"But we can't afford to take any chances, can we, sir? And there's nothing else we can do."

"Nothing, but pray," I said succinctly. "And I doubt whether that will have any effect now."

"And keep on fighting, sir," the other added as I swung myself up onto the wing, felt my feet slipping on the ice which had already begun to form, with a loose powdering of snow on top making it even more treacherous. "Sooner or later, we're all going to pack up, through no fault of our own."

"You've got a point there, I suppose," I conceded. With an effort, I climbed into the cockpit, strapped my helmet beneath my chin, and tried to settle my body comfortably in the cramped and confined space. The air was bitterly cold and the metal felt chill against my body.

Less than five minutes had passed since the warning alarm had sounded and already, the messages were beginning to flash between the control tower and ourselves out there in the solitary, white loneliness of the blizzard-whipped airfield.

There was no point in maintaining radio silence now to confuse the approaching enemy, they knew almost exactly where they were to a couple of miles. Flying blind by radar, they could pick out the sprawling cities and estuaries beneath them, even through dense cloud and although the thick snowstorm might make it a little more difficult for them to pick out their position accurately, there was no doubt that they could do it without having to rely on our radio signals.

I found myself shivering violently from the cold and the excitement. Carefully, I pulled the cover of the cockpit over my head, shutting out the freezing wind. Outside, as I started the engine, feeling the shaking vibration tear through the shuddering airframe, I caught a glimpse of the ground crew, edging away from the plane, their figures partly obliterated by the snow which seemed to be thickening with every passing minute.

Where their wasted, sleep-exhausted bodies got the strength and endurance to continue, it was impossible to tell. Miraculously, they stood there with the wind and storm raging about them, seemingly impregnable.

Then there was a sudden flashing of green, just visible in the darkness. The instrument board shook faintly, quivering. The propeller turned over slowly as the engine coughed once or twice, then gathered momentum until it was a faintly-shining blur, scarcely visible.

The chocks were pulled away from beneath the wheels, the plane moved forward, gently at first, then gathering speed and the dark figures of the two men were lost in the world of whiteness behind the fighter's tail.

Quite suddenly, almost before I was aware of it, I was alone in the darkness. There was nothing but the plane and the stretching whiteness of the snow around me. Even though I knew that the other planes in the flight were moving forward into their respective positions, I could see nothing of them, as I craned my neck to look about me. The snow hid everything. The wind, swinging from the north-east caught the plane side-on as I turned around the perimeter track, marked out dimly by a slight diminution in colour and it seemed as though the plane could never hope to shake itself free of the gigantic press of air, thrusting against her from one side. It took every ounce of strength to keep her on an even keel, to prevent the port wing from lifting and flipping the machine over on its side.

Around me, the storm wielded its wild, inhuman hatred with a firce, unabating cunning The perimeter track turned slowly towards the far end of the runway. As the plane moved forward, the wind direction altered subtly, coming from a changing direction every minute. Conditions were worsening every second and it seemed incredible that the enemy could really be up there, battering their way through a storm of such demoniacal fury. But the warning alarm had sounded and there was nothing we could do but obey it .Inside, I felt a sudden surge of fury. If that warning had been a false alarm. If there was, in reality, nothing there . . .

CHAPTER II

Dying—We Destroy

Take-off was a danger, a discomfort and a desperate physical battle to keep the plane in level flight. The wind blew with tremendous, bone-shaking force from starboard, so that it was impossible to head the plane right into it until the wheels had lifted clear of the ground, and only then with the maximum of risk. The green light from Control was still flashing intermittently over on the port bow, just visible as the remaining planes rose clear of the ground and gained height slowly.

It was almost impossible to fly into that terrible wind, the engine strained and the airspeed indicator was far lower than it should have been. Ice was forming slowly on the wings but at the moment, it was not particularly dangerous.

We climbed slowly to three thousand feet and circled the airfield. Down below there was a deep darkness as we lifted through the swarming clouds. Overhead, once we had reached out predetermined height and were flying steadily through the upper fringes of the storm, it was not a completely dark night.

The clouds were not as thick here and it was just possible to see through them, above them, both in front and on either side. Patches of dense black sky showed, littered with a powdering of frosty stars, brilliantly clear whenever the scudding clouds broke sufficiently, but obscured again within seconds as the shrieking, drifting storm passed over us again, blotting out everything.

Slowly, we turned on course, heading in a direction which would take us parallel to Kassel some twenty miles in the distance to the east, keeping our height. Most of the blizzard was below us, with scarcely five hundred feet of cloud above us and five minutes later, we climbed above the topmost layer of cloud and came out into the clear sky. Gone now, were the snow-laden clouds, although the wind was still as fierce, tossing the plane about the sky as though it were a cork on some stormy sea.

I glanced down, over the metal edge of the cockpit. Below, there were only mountainous masses of dark grey cloud, broken and confused in places, breaking this way and that as the gale-force wind caught them, but always tending to drive them southwards. Some of these great mountains of darkness—by no stretch of the imagination was it possible to call them clouds, in the strict sense of the word, towered to several thousand feet, cluttering up the horizon so that even here, the stars were lost to view. Fortunately, these all seemed to lie to the south of our position and we could afford to ignore them completely.

"Either they're flying blind, below the cloud, or they aren't coming and that alarm meant nothing," said a voice over the intercom which I recognised instantly as belonging to Hausser.

"Some heads will roll if it was a false alarm." There was a note of anger in Jensen's voice as he cut in on the other. A pause, then he went on viciously: "Can't see a damned thing through this cockpit. The storm seems to have scoured it completely."

Reluctantly, I forced myself upright in my seat, peered about me. The plastic of the cockpit was pitted and scarred, I realised, probably by the incessant pounding which it had received over the last dozen flights when even the slightest amount of ice in the air, driven at the terrific speeds of the storm, would have roughened it sufficiently to reduce the clarity of vision to what it was now.

No searchlights were visible from that height. Even had they been burning down there around Kassel, it was doubtful whether we could have seen them through that dense murk which writhed and boiled below us. The blackness was deep and complete.

"Enemy aircraft. Just on the horizon, bearing oh-five-oh." Eberbach's voice was sharp, higher pitched than usual, alive with sudden excitement. Even his weariness seemed to have been forgotten in this new discovery.

"Can't see anything." Jensen's voice was calmer, steadier over the intercom. "Are you sure?"

"Positive." There was no mistaking the tone of almost agitated conviction in the other's voice. "I can still see them, but their course is taking them slightly away from us."

"Then they can't be heading for Kassel," I said briefly, glancing through the scoured plastic of the cockpit. A moment later, I caught a fragmentary glimpse of the formation of black dots, just visible with averted vision, outlined against the greyness of the foaming clouds. When I turned my head to look directly at them, they faded tantalisingly into the general greyness of the background.

"Circling well to the west," went on Jensen morosely. "That could still mean that they intend to attack Kassel, but they're at a slightly lower altitude than we are. Climb to five thousand feet and take up an interception course. They'll have to go down through that blizzard if they're to drop their bombs with any degree of accuracy and that might be our chance to attack them before they're aware of our presence."

"What if they decide to use radar and bomb from a high altitude?" interrupted Eberbach.

"That's a chance we'll just have to take. Off-hand, I'd say that they outnumber us by four-to-one. We might not get a second chance unless we can keep the advantage of surprise."

We turned, headed onto the new course which would

bring us into contact with the enemy bomber force. Almost dead ahead now, slightly over on the port bow, there was no mistaking them, even from that distance. They were Lancasters all right, but there seemed to be no fighter escort although it was possible that the enemy could have provided one, operating from closer at hand, from one of the captured airfields in France.

There had been a time when we had flown the black unfriendliness of the night sky with a feeling of excitement in our bodies, tensed and expectant, prowling the dark hills of the clouds until we had located the enemy, hunting our prey, destroying the Spitfires and Hurricanes over their own territory so that our bombers might go in unhindered except for the guns on the ground. Then we had been addicted to the task of destruction, men born to kill, and it was a job we could handle with ease.

But that had been a couple of years ago and hundreds of miles away over the southern counties of England or the moon-washed coastal waters off France and the Low Countries. I could feel the weariness in my mind as well as in my ice-cold body. It never left me now, not these days.

Instinctively, I increased the power to the engine, lining the plane up on the black dots in the distance, glancing back at the instrument panel, to the enemy bombers again, sideways through the cockpit canopy to the rest of the flight, still in formation, still holding course in spite of the buffeting of the wind.

A good pilot had to have eyes all over his head, to be able to take in a multitude of things in a few seconds and store the facts away in his brain for future reference. Nothing could be allowed to distract him and it was essential that nothing should be missed. But very few of us were *good* pilots now. Weariness had dragged at our minds, there was a deeply-seated, lethargic fatigue in our bodies and reflexes, once swift and instinctive, were slower now. That was why, even morning, fewer of us came back.

Not so much because of the numerical superiority of the enemy, nor of their planes, nor even because of our own patched-up machines which were, inevitably, so inferior to those of the British; but because we were no longer quick-thinking creatures capable of swift decisions and put them into action equally swiftly and decisively.

The black specks were no longer featureless dots. Time had speeded up, was moving faster now. The enemy bombers kept on course, giving no indication that they had spotted us.

The intercom remained silent now. The enemy had been sighted and that was all we needed. I began to experience a rising sensation of tense anticipation in my body building up inside the pit of my stomach, knotting the muscles almost painfully. It wasn't the lust to kill but something closely akin to it; the feeling of a man whose business, whose entire life was dedicated to destruction.

There was nothing personal about it at all and in a way, that was the worst thing about it. There were men inside those bombers, men with hopes and fears similar to my own, doing their duty as I was and no matter how hard I tried, I failed to convince myself that I actually enjoyed killing them.

"Enemy opening fire. Taking evasive action!" Jensen's voice sounded harsh and urgent.

I turned my head slightly, saw the flickering streams of light immediately. The four-engined bombers were already turning away, breaking formation slightly.

Less than ten seconds later, one of the Lancasters moved across my sights. Swinging the plane slightly, I kept the dark image there, squeezing the firing button, firing a short, exploratory burst. The lines of tracer lashed out into the darkness, closed the distance between the bomber and myself.

Almost absently, I noticed that the brief burst had passed under the swaying bomber, missing by less than five feet. Again, I lifted the nose of the fighter by a fraction, fired again. In that fraction of a second, the bomber, weaving about the sky, had taken evasive action and was already beginning to slip out of the sights. As it thundered by, less than a hundred yards away, with the distance opening slightly, I saw the tracer eating into its metal side, being swallowed by the dark fuselage, almost without effect.

Even as the shells smashed into the enemy plane, it

dipped away violently on one wing-tip, heading downwards into the cloud which was its only cover. I followed it down urgently, feeling the blood pounding in my ears, aware that my fingers were gripping the stick with a desperate eagerness.

The fighter responded valiantly. Two seconds passed, three, four—and still the Lancaster went down, swinging from side to side in an effort to shake me off. Cloud thickened around me, blotting it out for long moments at a time; a vaguely-seen shape, weaving violently in an attempt to escape destruction.

Tension, over-anxiety, blended with a little fear, all battled for supremacy in my mind and I felt a sudden stab of apprehension. Coolness of nerve was essential at a time like this. The slightest misjudgement could mean all the difference between success and failure; and there was always the possibility that the enemy gunners were striving to get me in their sights.

I could see nothing of the rest of the flight, although they were around somewhere, picking their individual targets from the broken formation. Three thousand feet and I suddenly came out into a clear patch again, the clouds fled away in tattered strips and I could see the enemy bomber clearly, heading straight towards me, less than three hundred yards away.

Whether it was a deliberate manoeuvre on the part of the enemy pilot, or an accidental change of course, carried out precipitously by a rattled man, but the sudden appearance of the bomber, looming large directly in front of me, almost unnerved me completely.

It was so utterly unexpected—and there is nothing more nerve-wracking than to see another plane, huge and threatening, looming massively, terrifyingly over the open sights of your own guns and know that, except for a miracle, you have less than the time taken for a couple of heartbeats to live.

Madly, I banked to the right to avoid the almost inevitable collision, my thumb jamming down instinctively on the firing button as I did so. The Lancaster slid by in the darkness, obliquely, the nearer wing-tip barely scraping mine. Less than a foot separated us in that single, terrifying, blood-freezing instant. A moment later, there was a sudden, vicious burst of orange flame, slipping swiftly by at the edge of my vision.

It was gone in an instant and the next moment, there was only blackness around me and the clouds beginning to roll in again, blotting everything out. Swiftly, I swung the plane around in a steep, banking circle, turning back, striving to pick out the enemy bomber through the thickening cloud.

My first conscious thought was the numbing appreciation that my wing-tip had caught that of the Lancaster, shearing through metal and wire. Hard on the heels of that thought came the shocking realisation that this couldn't possibly be the explanation. I would have felt the shock of the impact, transmitted through the plane and into my body. The only other possibility was that my shells had struck home and hit a vital part of the enemy aircraft, possibly one of the fuel-tanks, or even the bomb-bay, detonating the high-explosive in the bombs.

I shook my head to clear it, caught a glimpse of something burning on the starboard bow, almost a thousand feet below me. I went down, through the upper layers of clouds until I could pick it out clearly. It was the Lancaster, there was no doubt about that. The nose of the bomber was pointed straight down, the fuselage turning slightly about its longitudinal axis, one wind sheared off almost at the base.

Even as I watched, there was an instantaneous, blinding flash of gasoline flame and the bomber was no longer a machine, but a torn and flaming mass of scattered wreckage that plunged earthwards, fading slowly. There were no blossoming parachutes.

My face felt cold as I pulled back on the stick, climbed back to five thousand feet. The enemy formation was well scattered now, some heading towards Kassel which was their primary objective, others trying to head downwards into the cloud which covered most of the ground. The blizzard was still raging down there, although here, at five thousand feet, the stars were clear and frosty in a black sky.

Running directly into the wind now, the plane was

amazingly steady, holding course to an almost fantastic degree when I recalled the force of the wind down on the ground. Ice was still forming slowly on the wings, but gradually, the effect was becoming noticeable. The airspeed indicator was dropping slowly in spite of any attempt to increase speed.

Minutes dragged by slowly as I hunted for the remnants of the enemy squadron. Occasionally, something would go down in flames in the distance, but it was too dark and too far away to tell whether it was a British bomber or a German fighter. I caught only fleeting glimpses of the other planes in the darkness, then quickly lost them again against the black, seething mass of the clouds.

I banked and headed east towards Kassel. Ominously, nothing came through over the intercom. For some reason, the others were maintaining radio silence. For two, perhaps three minutes, I flew on a level keel—it seemed far longer than that, but not long enough for any aircraft to show up against the darkness—and then a diffuse glow was suddenly apparent almost directly beneath me.

Several seconds fled before I realised what it was—a great mass of fire where the enemy bombs had turned the city into a raging holocaust. It was soon obvious that they were bombing from a high level, using their sensitive radar technique, keeping well above the cloud layer where they were safe from the anti-aircraft guns sited around Kassel.

And then, as if a film had been shifted from in front of my eyes, I could make out the dark, swiftly-moving shapes around me, clearly visible by averted vision.

I felt fiercely, strangely excited and happy. To hell with their numerical superiority, I thought savagely, if the searchlights and anti-aircraft guns could not get them, at least we could. I could see the bombers clearly now, silhouetted against the vague glow beneath the clouds. This was war as I liked to fight it. Weariness was temporarly forgotten. Some of the old, warm exhilaration was coming back, making itself dominant in my mind, driving away the cold and apathy. This was not the normal cat-and-mouse kind of battle, fraught with the hide-and-seek frustration of chasing the enemy through the clouds, trying to outguess him. This was war in the open where I could see the bombers and do everything in my power to destroy them.

Inwardly, I knew that this same kind of feeling had invaded the minds of the rest of the men. No longer did we care for ourselves. Instead, we looked upon ourselves as avengers for the destruction which had been wrought down below. We remembered the men and women and children who would inevitably have been killed by that rain of high explosives which had caused those fires whose extent could only be guessed at by what we saw from above.

This was the part of flying which made it really worth-while to be alive. Now I was in a world which had very little in common with that several thousand feet below, where the snow was beginning to cover everything, where men stood and shivered in the biting, arctic wind that drove needles of pain through their limbs and froze the blood in their veins, where eyes strained to pick out details through a blinding curtain of snow and the pain of re-turning circulation was somehow worse than the numb-ness, the lack of feeling, which preceded it.

Here, there were the bright stars around me, a few of them caught and dimmed slightly by high wisps of cirrus, but most of them brilliant and clear, forming themselves into long, trailing constellations. Occasionally, there would be a cloud higher than the rest, building up from the rippling mass which covered the ground, standing out in pale silver on the horizon, but for the most part, the cloud lay below me, soft and smooth, moving only with the motion of the aircraft.

It was hard to remember that, even here, in this seemingly serene and calm setting, there was danger. Danger from fatigue which made it difficult to spot the enemy planes until they were close enough to open fire; danger from the sub-zero air around me, depositing its moisture in the form of an ever-thickening layer of ice on the wings and tail unit, increasing the weight and the drag.

I eased a cramped leg, stretched it gently in the con-fined space of the cockpit. There was a black shadow, swift-moving and vast, a little distance away off the port bow. My mind rolled over once in my head, realisation came in a brief flash of clarity, and in that same instant, four streams of red tracer like frozen splinters of fire, rushed out of the starlit darkness, converging on me. The battle suddenly became a very personal thing for me.

Miraculously, I escaped without serious damage. The enemy fire had been almost spot on the target, high, but not quite high enough. It seemed to waver, steadied, then dipped out of sight under the fighter's nose. Almost before it had swept past me, I had put the plane into a tight sweep, twisting instinctively in evasive action, turning on one wing-tip. Metal creaked and groaned under the stress imposed upon it.

Seconds later, I came up behind the enemy bomber, lining up to starboard of his tail, keeping to one side of the deadly rear turret which was suddenly hammering away in my direction. Wing down, plane level, straight and steady.

Action was purely automatic now. I was part of the plane itself, an automaton. A burst from the Lancaster reached out with frantic urgency. It was close, a little on the high side, but dangerously close. I corrected course quickly, held on grimly behind the other, heard the screeching rattle of metal rasping through metal.

The fighter was hit, but still responding well to the controls so it was doubtful whether it had been anything serious. Whatever it was, it would have to be investigated later. There was no time now. I squeezed the firing button. The wing guns thundered and screamed. I held them on the target for a full five seconds.

There were men inside that plane, frightened, apprehensive men; but I was past thinking about them. It was the plane itself that I was after, nothing else.

A ball of red flame spilled out from the fuselage, immediately aft of the wings. Swiftly, it spread outwards, engulfing the bomber almost completely so that only the tips of the stretching wings and the tail unit miraculously survived. There was nothing else but this huge ball of fire, terrifying and heart-stopping in its immensity.

The black smoke began to pour from the stricken plane and a few moments later, the nose went down and she disintegrated completely a hundred feet or so below me. The oily, black smoke, flattening out behind the plane, rolled about me for an instant as I flew through it, thick and impenetrable.

For the next two hours, in the darkness and the clouds, we played cat-and-mouse with the returning Lancasters, intercepting them as they tried to flee after dropping their loads of high explosive, firing at them occasionally, spotting them briefly, tantalisingly, through breaks in the clouds.

CHAPTER III

The Price of Victory

Down through the wind-driven clouds, where they thinned out at less than eight hundred feet, the airfield was now indistinguishable from the surrounding countryside, everything lying beneath a sheet of white. It was still dark, almost four o'clock in the morning, and only the hedges showed up clearly as straight, intersecting black lines against the snow. The beacon on the hill to the south of the airfield was just visible if one knew where to look for it. During the first half of the run-in I had missed it entirely, then I caught the faint glimmer as I dropped lower and it was just possible to make out the lights along the runway in use.

Now that everything was almost finished, the fatigue which had never been very far away, was making itself felt. My eyelids were like lead and there seemed to be a faint red haze dancing in front of my eyes, making it difficult to pick out details clearly. With an effort, I held the plane steady on course. The wind still blew from the side, dangerously strong, seeking to turn the nose of the machine off-course, away from the runway.

The snow was thinning, but still heavy enough to partially obscure the buildings on the edge of the perimeter track as I felt the wheels touch, heard the faint bleat of tortured rubber, felt the momentary slide as the brakes came on gently. Then I was down, the plane still responding to the controls, although more sluggishly than earlier.

I reached the end of the runway, turned and taxied slowly around the perimeter track. There was something weird, almost uncanny about the stretching whiteness of the airfield around me, the utter absence of movement in all that open space. Two of the other planes were already down before me and were standing in front of the hangar, the mechanics already working on them in spite of the weather.

Wearily, I switched off the engine, felt the silence hit at my ears, and suddenly realised just how tired I really was. Slipping back the canopy, I felt the sudden chill as the cold air swirled in around me. All feeling of warmth vanished from my body. For a long moment, I sat there in the cockpit, staring at the instrument panel, gasping for breath.

Another three hours to dawn and by all the signs, it would be another wild and terrible dawn. Overhead, the lowering clouds swept by barely a hundred feet high and the snow coming in whirling gusts. With an effort, I pulled myself out of the cockpit, stood for a moment on the wing of the plane, gasping as the wind brinded me with ice and cold. My fingers were numbed immediately and I beat them together in a vain attempt to bring the circulation back.

Hastily, I pulled the collar of my greatcoat up, clambered down to the ground. The two ground-crew men came running forward out of the darkness, their entire bodies swathed like mummies against the cold.

"Good morning, sir," muttered Sergeant Herschmann. "How was it up there?"

"You wouldn't believe me even if I told you. When you get above this murk, you can see for miles. No snow, stars like fire; ice in plenty though, but nothing like this."

"They bombed Kassel again, sir."

"I know. We spotted them well to the west. Managed to shoot several down, but it was inevitable that some of them should get through."

"Some of the preliminary reports have just started coming through, sir," interrupted the other man. "Seems they hit the city pretty badly. Destruction at the marshalling yards was almost total. There won't be much rail traffic moving through to the front for several days."

"I know, I know." I nodded wearily. My mind seemed dazed almost to the point where I could think of nothing clearly. "If only some of these people who're always shouting about the Lutwaffe went up there some time in weather like that, and saw what it was really like, I'm sure there would be fewer complaints. By the way, you'd better take a good look at the plane. They scored a couple of lucky hits and although it didn't seem to be anything serious, you'd better give it as complete an overhaul as you can."

"We'll take a look at it as soon as it's light, sir," murmured the Sergeant. His voice was a husky, tired whisper, scarcely heard above the thin wailing of the wind.

"What about the others? Are they all down yet?"

"Two planes landed less than ten minutes ago, sir. They seemed all right. The others are still up there somewhere. Did we lose any during the fighting?"

"I've no idea, I'm afraid." My teeth were chattering uncontrollably in my head and huge, racking spasms seemed to be working their way through my body, until it was shaking terribly. My hands and feet seemed no longer to be part of my body.

"Something coming in now, sir." The other man pointed, lifting his head momentarily against the biting teeth of the wind.

I turned my head slightly, shielded my eyes against the needle-like gusts which battered us from every conceivable direction. For a long moment, it was impossible to make out anything. The Sergeant, close beside me, was muttering something to himself in the darkness, the words too faint to catch. His face, shockingly grey, haggard and splotched in places with threatened frostbite, was held rigidly forward as he peered into the blackness.

The airfield seemed curiously empty now and for some strange reason, I felt oddly alone, even with the presence of the two men beside me. Then, above the shrieking howl of the wind in my ears, I heard it; faintly at first, but gradually growing louder until it was unmistakable.

The drone of an aircraft coming in to land. I screwed up my eyes in a desperate attempt to pick out the shape of the approaching plane. The blackness of the scudding clouds was unrelieved by any shape at all and for several seconds I could see nothing.

It was then that I noticed for the first time, a flickering flame in the distance, coming closer, swinging a little from side to side. There was the rising roar of the Messerschmitt, at maximum throttle, coming in on a shallow dive.

"My God, he's on fire!" Vaguely, I was aware of the fact that I was yelling the words at the top of my voice, gripping the Sergeant tightly by the arm. The shape of the crippled fighter loomed up out of the featureless darkness. He was aligned on the runway, but the pilot was fighting desperately to keep the plane under control. The fire had started somewhere along the base of the starboard wing and was spreading rapidly throughout the whole length of the plane, fanned by the tremendous force of the wind, whipping the licking flames along the metal.

There seemed little hope that the plane could land safely in her condition. Quite suddenly, the sky opened up in front of my startled gaze in a widening flare of actinic, coruscating light, dazzling my vision, making tear-filled eyes narrow against its shocking flare. So intense, so extraordinarily brilliant was that glare that it hurt my eyes and my pupils contracted so violently that the night seemed twice as dark as before when I hastily averted my vision.

Then, with an effort, I forced myself to look back as the fighter, flattening out and still under partial control, pancaked onto the runway at the far end, skidded slightly to one side, slid forward on its crumpling undercarriage for several hundred yards, carried forward by its own terrible momentum; a flaming torch, a burning tomb for the man inside.

Instinctively, I screwed up my eyes as the sudden sound of the explosion reached my eyes above the roaring of the wind, catching my breath in sudden dismay. In the distance, less than three seconds later, the fire tender sped soundlessly across the airfield towards the fire, the noise of its powerful engine and the wail of its warning siren whipped away by the wind, so that neither could be heard by us as we stood there, scarcely able to move, our bodies frozen into immobility by the shock and sub-zero cold.

Behind the fire-tender, came the ambulance, but one glance at the rising flames of that funeral pyre was enough to tell me that it would not be needed. If the pilot, whoever he was, was still alive, he had only seconds to live in that inferno.

"Let's get over there," I said urgently. "There may be something we can do. At least we might be able to find out who it is."

There wasn't a chance, of course, and I knew even as I spoke, that I lied in my teeth, that it was only wishful thinking on my part. But anything was better than standing there, watching the petrol-driven flames eating viciously through the twisted metal of the wreckage.

The airfield looked wide, wider than I had imagined as I began to run across it, feet slipping, sliding on the snow-covered grass, gasping, pushing, falling and then heaving myself to my feet, only to fall again a split second later, with the breath rasping harshly in my lungs.

My mouth felt dry, my tongue cleaving to the roof and the backs of my teeth. I ran with fear and apprehension in my mind, urging my flagging feet forward as nothing else could, making me forget temporarily the painful leadenness in my legs, the biting pain in my air-starved lungs and the stinging bite of the knife-edged wind that whipped the tails of my heavy coat around my back and legs so fiercely that every individual slap was like the thud of a mighty hand.

We ran through the snow. Blood throbbed and pounded agonisingly at the back of my temples and my vision wavered and blurred with tears, whipped up by the wind. There was the acrid, choking smell of smoke from the burning wreckage in my nostrils. Shaking my head numbly, I forced my eyes to remain open. Heat singed my hair and face as I moved cautiously forward. The fire-tender had drawn up to one side of the plane and three men were dragging a long hose towards it, struggling through the snow, trying to hold on to the heavy, reinforced rubber with fingers that, even in the heavy, protective gloves, held no feeling.

"Watch for the ammunition," I shouted. The men ran forward to within a couple of yards of the burning plane. "There may still be shells on board the plane."

Vaguely, I saw one of the men turn at my sudden shout. It was obvious that he had not understood what I had yelled, for he merely waved a gloved hand, moved forward another couple of inches and signalled to the men in the fire-tender to begin pouring foam onto the wreckage.

"For God's sake, keep away." I raised my voice until my throat was hoarse. "There's nothing you can do for the pilot now."

In my mind's eye, I could visualise the flames, already completely out of hand, eating their way avidly towards the fuel tank and the belts of ammunition in the wing cannon. Drawing in a single breath, I watched as the first stream of white foam splashed out of the hose and fell into the raging furnace in the heart of the plane. For a moment, it seemed as though they were going to make it in spite of the fury of the fire, fed by the fierce through draught of the keening wind.

Outlined against the flames, the fuselage, struts and wing sections had been bent and buckled into weird shapes by the intense heat. Amidships, the gasoline-fed flames still beat and leapt at the dark heavens, blown to one side, incinerating everything inside the body of the fighter.

There was no sign of the pilot. The fury of the flames was such, that he must have been burned to a cinder within minutes of the crash. Metal melted and dripped as though under the influence of some gigantic blow-torch which had cleanly stripped the thinner metal from the outer sections, exposing the interior.

The men from the fire-tender, freezing one minute and reeling back with the intense heat the next, fought their way to within a few feet of the furnace, utterly regardless of their own safety. It was impossible to see their frames, muffled up against the shrieking wind, or to wonder whether or not they knew that any hope of saving the pilot was gone, had been futile for almost five minutes.

Two of the men edged their way forward towards the cockpit which was still recognisable against the leaping flames. Then, almost before I was aware of their intention, they had leapt forward, tearing at the buckled canopy of the cockpit with their gloved hands, oblivious of the danger from exploding ammunition or fuel tanks, the gloves peeling from their fingers. Still they tugged at the twisted metal with their bare hands and when they finally fell back from the flames, they had something with them, something charred and virtually unrecognisable, a twisted shape which might have been a human being, but for the way in which they carried it between them as they stumbled hurriedly away from the wreckage.

I shut my eyes as they lurched forward past me, the wind whipping the hoods of their uniforms back from their faces, so that I could make out, by the flickering light of the fire, their features twisted with shock and pain.

Swiftly, I turned and ran back. A boiling column of red-shot flame leapt up into the air, streaking more than twenty-five feet towards the clouds as a tremendous detonation tore the heart out of the stricken plane and blazing wing sections went spinning off into the darkness.

It had to come, my mind screamed at me. The time for caution was past. Another minute and everything would go up and there were still planes to come in to land; and the runway was virtually blocked. Behind me, there seemed to be complete confusion. Someone was shouting vague orders and there was the harsh shrilling of a whistle being blown at irregular intervals. Fighting for breath, I flung myself forward at the same instant as the main fuel tanks went up. Then there was no time to think of anything else, no time to turn my head and look around, or even to prepare myself.

The air was suddenly savage with the violence of the detonation wave, filled with twisted strips of metal, cutting through the wind. My ears were ringing with the vast, boiling roar that beat savagely across the airfield, streaking the snow and the night sky with rising pillars of red and orange flame.

The smoke, thick and convoluted, rose up into the wind-driven, scudding clouds, mingled with them and hung as a dense pall over everything, lit from beneath by the flashes of man-created lightning as the ammunition exploded.

I lifted my head and slitted my eyes against the glare. A stream of red arrows flashed across my line of vision and vanished into the darkness. Tracer spat in thin lines of red fire, hurtling in all directions. For a couple of seconds, I lay where I had fallen, thrown to the ground by the violence of the blast, all of the breath knocked out of my body. A tremor of sheer panic hit me for the next moment or two. Then it was all over.

Cautiously, I lifted my head and looked behind me. What was left in the middle of the runway no longer resembled a plane. By no conceivable stretch of the imagination could it possibly called a Messerschmitt.

Slowly, we got to our feet and surveyed the scene, scarcely feeling the icy chill which laid its hand on our bodies. The entire plane had been destroyed. The fire was dying down slowly, the metal of the tail unit turning black in the intense cold. One of the men had been hit by the last and lay moaning on the snow, his hands held over his ears as though to shut out the dreadful noise of that vast explosion.

Sergeant Herschmann did not even spare me a glance as he ran forward and went down on one knee beside the injured man, turning him over gently.

"Carl!" he called loudly, shaking the other a little. His voice, a voice which I noticed impersonally was cracked and quivering slightly with strain, echoed strangely on the wind.

"Carl! Is anything the matter?"

The injured man stirred a little and moaned softly. Going down beside him, I called to one of the other men to bring a torch so that we might take a good look at his injuries.

Slowly, with a clumsy deliberation, I peeled off my gloves, sucked hard on my teeth as the icy wind drove all of the feeling out of my fingers, and reached an exploratory hand towards the other's head. It came away wet and sticky and I glanced down at it in mild surprise. A moment later, one of the ambulance men came running forward, flashed the beam from his torch on the scene. By its light I caught a glimpse of the terrible gash in the side of the man's head. His hair was matted thickly with blood and his cap had fallen off, revealing the open wound from which the blood was still pumping slowly and regularly. It trickled slowly down the side of his face, along the folds of his skin and onto the snow where it spread an ominous red stain on the ground.

"He's been hit by a flying piece of metal," I said thickly. "Must have caught him a glancing blow, but there's just the possibility that it's fractured his skull. He's barely conscious which is a good thing, I suppose, otherwise the pain would have been far too much for him to bear."

Herschmann glanced up at the orderly. "Do we have any morphia at all that we can give him?"

The other hesitated. Very little, I'm afraid, Sergeant. We brought some out for the pilot of that plane, but—" he paused, licked his lips, and the light of the torch wavered more violently than before as though a wave of agitated apprehension had seized him, "—but somehow, I don't think he'll be needing it."

I nodded grimly towards the smoking wreckage of the Messerschmitt which several men were busy trying to remove from the runway, tugging at it with asbestos gloves. "Judging from that, I doubt whether there'll be enough left of him to identify him."

"Get that morphia," said Herschmann harshly. There was a peculiar quality to his voice which I couldn't identify.

The orderly was back within a minute. Carefully, he plunged the needle into the injured man's arm, held it there for a long moment, then withdrew it and pulled down the sleeve of the thick tunic.

"He'll be a little easier now," he said thinly, "until we can get him back into the hospital. That's a nasty wound he's got there. He's lucky to be still alive."

I got to my feet and stood swaying for a moment, feeling the wind tearing at my body, trying its utmost to throw me down. Gradually, I became aware of the fact that Sergeant Herschmann was standing beside me, looking at me out of the corner of his eye; and there was a strange, almost pleading look on his face.

"Do you mind if I go in the ambulance with him, sir?" He licked his lips. "You won't be needing me any more tonight and I'll see to the overhaul first thing tomorrow morning."

I looked at him for a long second, his shoulders hunched and his head held low. "What's got into you, Sergeant?" I asked. "There seems to be something here I know nothing about. Why do you want to go with this man to the hospital?"

"I—it's just that this man, sir . . . well, he's—"

"He's what, Sergeant?"

"He's my brother, sir."

CHAPTER IV

Night Intruders

Shortly after midday on the following day was the only possible time for a burial. The ice had turned the earth into iron and the party of men detailed for the burial group had a hard time digging the four graves in the nearby churchyard. The pilot who had died when his plane crashed in flames on the runway had been a youngster of nineteen, named Heinrich Müller. A veteran then, in spite of his years, who had been with the Squadron for close on seventeen months and had flown almost as many missions as the rest of us. Like all of us, he was living on borrowed time and his death had been virtually inevitable.

Later, that morning, before the grey dawn, three more planes had crashed on the airfield, two because they had come in onto the wrong runway in the darkness, their sense of direction baffled by the snow sweeping thickly over the ground. Visibility when they had landed, had been less than ten feet, and there were low hills to the west of the airfield, lying in wait for the unwary. In some strange, unpredictable way, they had missed the hills in spite of the fact that they lay directly in their path, and had both hit the airfield, slightly to one side of the cross-wind runway, in almost the same spot within ten minutes of each other. There had been no chance for the first man.

He had been thrown clear by the force of the impact and when the rescuers had found him, some ten yards from the burning wreckage of the plane, there had not been a single mark on his body; only the peculiar twist of his neck and the empty, frightening lolling of his head told their own terrible story.

Spengler, the other pilot had landed ten minutes later in the middle of a blinding snowstorm, his petrol supply almost finished. There had been scarcely any fire and as he had used up virtually all of his ammunition, there was little danger from that score too.

When he had been pulled from the shattered cockpit, he had just been conscious, mumbling softly to himself, his face twisted into a grimace of pain. He had died of his internal injuries shortly after six o'clock on that grey and bitterly cold morning; and at almost the same instant as he died, the last of the planes came in, badly shot up.

The pilot obviously tried to do his best with the plane, but standing there outside the Control Building, it was painfully certain that he would be unable to hold it on course. I caught only glimpses of the plane, coming in low and far too fast. The usual practice was to make a single circuit of the airfield and then turn in on the appropriate runway.

To land a plane in darkness under normal conditions was difficult; to land crosswind in a raging snowstorm was highly hazardous; but to bring in a plane that had been shot to pieces and to land it by guesswork in the snow and the greyness of an early dawn was a suicidal impossibility. The slightest miscalculation on the part of a tired, and possibly wounded, pilot could be fatal.

The plane had hit the end of the runway at an angle, skidded on its belly for almost fifty yards before slewing to a grinding halt. Miraculously, there had been no fire. The plane had remained substantially upright and the foam extinguishers had not to be used. But the pilot was dead when they brought him out of the cockpit; killed not by the force of the crash, not by the bone-shuddering impact and the deceleration, but by the five bullets in his chest, fired from one of the British bombers.

Now, we stood by the open graves in the wind-swept

graveyard, unmoving, the intense numbness eating into our muffled bodies. One by one, the four coffins were lowered into the earth and were gone. For long seconds after that, no one moved. The voice of the priest, husky and quiet, paused, spoke for another minute, then died away.

Even now, it seemed incredible that these men could be dead. Only twenty-four hours earlier, they had been alive like myself, knowing that death would come to someone in the near future, but not believing that it would ever come to them. Now it had come and those of us that were left, stood in the thin sleet and watched their mortal remains disappearing into the earth.

There was something unreal, almost hypnotic about that simple and soul-stirring ceremony. The honours were brief. It was a bitterly cold afternoon, with the wind shifting slightly to the south-west and the snow changing into sleet which beat at our faces and gummed up our eyes so that, in the end, it was almost impossible to see anything properly.

Shivering, we clustered around the graves, then stood there while they were filled with earth. There was an almost inaudible sigh, a straightening of the shoulders, as the task was finished. My brain seemed empty inside my head, my mind like a dark void, empty of all thought, as I walked beside Jensen along the narrow, winding, weedy pathway through the churchyard, the branches of the trees overhead, dripping moisture onto our heads.

"Very soon, if this continues, there won't be any of us left to continue the fight," I said slowly, putting my thoughts into words.

Jensen looked at me, silent, his face expressionless, then looked away again, staring straight ahead of him. Watching him, he seemed strangely different, his face set and stonily impassive, the face of a man forced to carry on under difficult, almost impossible conditions. As leader of the fighter squadron, he had over a score of lives in his keeping; and it was painfully obvious that he considered he had made one wrong decision too often.

"Is there no chance of getting any reinforcements, men or machines?"

Jensen, his face haggard, shook his head ponderously.

"None at all, I'm afraid." He rubbed some of the feeling back into his face with his gloved hand. "I've applied for more men and planes for the flight, Graeber has backed me up to the best of his ability, but the reserves are all dried up. The Luftwaffe is finished, but nobody wants to believe it. Maybe it sounds like treason speaking this way, but a man sometimes has to act according to his lights.

"But you can't help feeling antagonistic towards those higher up when you have to witness scenes like that almost every week. The men are tired, completely and utterly finished. You and I are the same, but somehow, God alone knows how, we can still manage to go up there and take everything that comes although there have been times, especially like last night, when I felt like throwing it in."

He looked incuriously at his gloved hands, holding them in front of him as though they were no longer a part of him, but something divorced from the rest of his body.

I caught the other's quick look and shrugged. "What the devil do they think we're doing? Surely they can't be expecting us to fight this way until the last man goes up in the last plane—and fails to come back again?"

Desperately, I tried to keep the anger out of my voice. We came out onto the main road and I looked about me at the terrible damage which had been caused by the bombing of the past few nights. This was the old part of Kassel, away from the main centre of the city. The railway ran through the tall, stately buildings some three-quarters of a mile away to the south and there, the bomb had, inevitably, been worse than elsewhere.

A wave of bitterness swept through me. The British had certainly aimed their loads of high explosives with a deadly accuracy, even with the cloud base at five hundred feet and the cover ten-tenths with snow and high wind. There was no doubt in my mind any longer that they must have been using newly perfected radar techniques in their bombing.

Jensen walked in silence beside me, our footsteps crunching on the gravel in companionable unison. He did not seem to have heard my last remark. How much longer was this one-sided battle going to last? The enemy could throw almost a thousand bombers at us in a single raid.

They no longer depended upon good weather before they attacked, indeed, they seemed to prefer launching their attacks during periods of bad weather or moonless nights, when we would be grounded and it would be virtually impossible for the searchlights to pick them up, or the batteries defending the city to line up on the targets flying high and above the cloud.

Perhaps, in their own stubborn, inflexible way, those who directed the operations of the Luftwaffe in these dark days, thought that we still stood a chance of defeating the R.A.F. and the tremendous armadas of Flying Fortresses sent over by the American Air Force, mainly during the hours of daylight. Maybe they considered that we were automatons, machines, instead of creatures of flesh and blood, needing proper food and rest to combat this round-the-clock bombing.

But these thoughts did not last for long in my tired mind. I walked beside the others, towards the truck at the end of the street, with long, quick steps, disregarding the aches and bruises in my body. Very soon, unless I was very much mistaken, the enemy would come over again. There would be no more rest for us and tomorrow, or the day after, we would stand there again, and see more of our companions lowered into the earth, their last resting place.

I glanced down at my watch. It was almost one-thirty. While the others climbed into the back of the truck, I slipped into the seat beside Jensen. In some strange way, I felt there was a quiet accusation in the silence of the others, and there returned that sense of guilt which had come to me several times before, a kind of weak and angry shame and, without meaning to, I blurted out savagely:

"You know, I sometimes get so goddamned sick and tired of this that I wonder whether all of these high and mighty principles were supposed to be fighting for, are really worth the trouble."

My immediate reaction was one of irritation, angered at myself for having thought it necessary to explain these things to Jensen. After all, I reasoned, it wasn't exactly our fault that the tide of war had turned against us, and we were fighting on the defensive like this with too few men and too few planes to ever hope to turn the invaders back before they destroyed our beautiful cities.

The other's lips twitched into a slightly cynical smile, showing his uneven teeth. He started up the engine, slipped it into gear. As we moved off into the almost deserted *autobahn*, he said softly: "Maybe they are worth it. Maybe while we are prepared to live for these ideals, others are prepared to die for them."

"Maybe. But everything seems so terribly pointless. We go up there night after night, we lose a handful of good men every time, and for what? They get through no matter how we try to prevent them." My voice was suddenly dry and harsh, the words rasping thickly from a throat that was raw with emotion.

"That's probably why Graeber seems to be taking this so hard," muttered the other. He handled the wheel of the speeding truck expertly. There was very little traffic here, even at this time of the afternoon. Only military vehicles were allowed on the roads now; the shortage of gasoline was acute now and none could be spared for the public.

I tried to fight down the sensation of apprehension in my stomach and once again, there was that feeling of resentment whenever I thought of Graeber without actually being in his presence. Time and time again, during the past few weeks, I had found myself wondering whether or not he knew what he was doing. Surely, it would be impossible for him not to see what was happening to the men under his command.

The men were flying now when they ought to have been grounded months ago. They could not be expected to fly and fight, night after night. It was a murderous, vicious circle with only one exit—death.

The less sleep you had, the more you were supposed to fly, and the more you flew, the tireder you became; and so it went on. And then, on top of it all, there was the terrible tension, building up inside your body and brain, blotting out everything but the fear and the coldness. Every single factor conspired to destroy a man, to beat down his will to live, to tear to shreds his ability and ambition to destroy the enemy.

I smiled at Jensen and there was only coldness and no mirth in it. "Send men out under such terrible conditions as last night, force them to fly without proper sleep, and you're asking for trouble. Big trouble. You'll deprive them of every shred of resistance, both mental and physical. It's inevitable."

I settled myself more comfortably in the seat of the truck as the other swerved to avoid the potholes and bomb craters in the road, the wheels gripping the rough, uneven surface precariously. Sitting back, watching the dark buildings, tumbled here and there in shattered heaps of brick and stone, slide past on either side, feeling, rather than seeing the strange quietness in the city, I tried to think things out, to put myself into the minds of other people, the men who really gave the orders. Were they such fanatics as they were made out to be? Did they really care nothing for the military and the machines we were now forced to use?

The two great western blocs now formed one of the most tremendous fighting forces the world had ever seen. They had established a firm foothold on the continent against all the predictions of the military experts and only the stunchest of idealists, only the most fanatical of the leaders failed to see that the end for Germany was in sight. The Russians, pouring in from the east could not be halted now. The British and Americans were pushing forward savagely in the west; and it seemed inevitable that they should meet somewhere close to Berlin.

We reached the outskirts of Kassel, left the scene of terrible destruction behind and drove slowly through the country lanes, back to the airfield.

I sat for a long moment in silence, listening abstractly to the muted voices of the men in the back of the truck as they talked and laughed among themselves. As far as Jensen was concerned, I knew there was little need for words between us. I knew him better than I had ever known any other man. Jensen, the man who had been flying with me since the beginning of the war, the man who was looked upon as a lucky leader for the flight. None of the enemy aircraft seemed able to touch him; from all of his missions, he had returned unharmed.

A lucky man, but how long could such fantastic luck last? Not for always, that was certain. Other men had seemed to be equally lucky and they had failed to come back from a mission at some time during their careers.

"I'll have another word with the Commandant when we get back," he said suddenly, breaking the silence. "These last few days have reduced the effective strength of the squadron almost to half. Something will have to be done if we're to remain an efficient fighting unit. Either they send us more trained pilots and machines, front-line aircraft, or we're as good as finished."

"I don't suppose you've any idea why they keep on wasting men and aircraft like this?"

Jensen pushed a cigarette into his mouth, lit it with one hand, keeping the other on the wheel, and blew a cloud of blue smoke in front of him. His words, when they came, growled through the smoke:

"I've no doubt that the orders come directly from the Reichmarshal himself. No one else would have the necessary authority to give such suicidal commands."

I lifted my shoulders wearily. "These last two weeks have done all of the damage. Before then, I'd have said that we might have held our own, against anything they could have thrown against us. Fourteen days of sheer, unadulterated hell with nothing to show for it except a city in shambles and nine men dead with as many machines written off completely. And every night, its the same thing, repeated over and over again. An eternity of cold and suffering and privation, fighting these front-line aircraft that the enemy keep sending over with machines that ought to have been scrapped a year ago. In the name of God, what do they think we are—machines?"

I thrust my hands deep into my pockets, felt the painful tingling of returning circulation. "They must realise that there's a limit to everything, to loyalty, and to human endurance. I'm surprised that we haven't lost far more men than we have. The men aren't to blame. You know yourself what it was like last night. They just can't help it. Tiredness can do strange things to a man if taken to the extreme. They can no longer think straight, they can't even tell right from wrong any longer.

"The only thing that can snap them out of it now is sleep, complete rest, relaxed rest free from the incessant danger. They'll give anything for that; but you know as well as I do that unless we get more reinforcements, it can never happen."

"I know, I know," said Jensen heavily. "I'll have another go at the Commandant as soon as we get back. I doubt whether it will do any good."

* * * *

Shivering in the sudden blast of icy air, I followed Jensen into the Commandant's office. The sudden summons had come as a surprise a few minutes after we had arrived back at the airfield.

Graeber pushed back his chair as we were shown in and began to pace restlessly across the room like an animal on a leash. Jensen and I glanced at each other, then looked back to the Commandant, and waited. For a moment, he continued to walk the floor and for all the attention he paid to us, we might not have existed Then he turned suddenly, strode back to his desk and lowered himself into his chair.

Wearily, he waved us to a couple of chairs and sat for a moment with his head bowed a little, his elbows resting on top of the desk, gazing sightlessly at his fingers.

Then he lifted his head tiredly, looked at us with eyes that were haunted by lack of sleep, smudged with purple shadows.

"I'm genuinely sorry about what happened last night and early this morning," he began quietly, his voice tightly. "Really sorry. They were all good men and it seems a pity that they should have to die like that, so futilely."

He paused, picked up his cigarette case from the desk and proffered it to us. I took one mechanically, lit it and leaned back in my chair. I could guess at what was coming next, the inevitable excuses, the condolences and, just for a moment, the familiar surge of anger swept through me, leaving my body and brain spent with the fierceness of the emotion. But the anger lasted only for a moment. I was too tried, really, far too weary to care.

"When I have to give the orders for men to go out night after night to meet the hordes of enemy bombers coming in from across the channel, I do so with the deepest regret; because, more than perhaps you realise, I'm deeply conscious of what you, and the rest of the men on this airfield, are going through at this particular time."

I coughed, waited until he had paused and glanced around, then said softly: "Why can't we have reinforcements, sir? Surely there must be some to spare in the country. They can't all have been sent to the Russian front and if it's so essential to save the armaments factories and marshalling yards from destruction, then we need all of the help we can get."

"I fully realise that," the other continued evenly, lighting his own cigarette. The flint wheel of his lighter made a sharp rasping sound in the momentary silence.

Leaning forward over the top of the desk, he went on: "Let us be perfectly frank with each other, gentlemen. The situation now is far worse than two, even one, month ago. Daily the enemy's air strength increases while our own, through no fault of ours, continues to diminish. Many times, I've asked for further men and planes. Every time, my request has been refused."

He paused, and spread his hands in a futile gesture. There was an expression of defeat on his broad features and a bleakness in his eyes which I had not noticed before. Now that I came to look at him closely, I saw several things which I had not previously suspected.

There were deep lines scored in the flesh of his cheeks and his face was grey, twisted occasionally into a grimace of helplessness.

"The reasons given for the refusal have varied, but in the main, they all add up to one thing. Germany doesn't have the planes or the men to spare. The factories can turn out only a limited amount of material and with every enemy attack, this is necessarily reduced. Our war effort, is slowly grinding to a halt and there seems to be nothing we can do about it."

Again, there was that note of helplessness in his tone and he stubbed out his cigarette with a purely mechanical motion, looking at the faint smear of ash on his fingertips with an expression of distaste.

There was no chance that he was overstating the situation, I thought dully, almost apathetically. Listening to his quiet, weary voice, it was impossible not to believe him, not to understand the full seriousness of our position. There was to be no let-up in our efforts. That was what would be coming next, I thought tiredly. This unequal, one-sided battle would continue until we were all killed or lying in some hospital bed with our limbs shattered or burned beyond all recognition.

And what did it all add up to in the end? Simply that the most we could do, the most anyone could do, would be to postpone the inevitable for a few more months. Germany could not be saved by some eleventh hour miracle. That much was certain. And the only trouble was that the people in command were either too foolish, or too blind, to see it.

"Do we just sit here and continue to throw our lives away, sir?" Jensen looked at the other steadily. "It all seems so very pointless, especially to us after just coming from the funeral of those four men."

The lashing bite in his voice failed to evoke any response. Graeber simply sat back a little tighter in his chair, his hands white-knuckled on the desk in front of him. Then he seemed to stir himself, tightening his lips into a hard, compressed line across the middle of his face.

"We don't sit here at all," he went on finally. "That's why I called you both in here." He picked up a sheaf of official documents from his desk, flicked through them for a moment, then continued:

"These are fresh orders received this morning. They come directly from Berlin, so there's no countermanding them, no chance of getting them altered or modified. It means that, for me, things will be even worse than before, although for both of you, they may be a little easier, I'm not sure."

"What are they, sir?"

Graeber was on his feet now, resting his weight on his arms, his fingers spread wide on the top of the desk. His eyes bored into ours.

"It seems I'm to lose half of you in the next two days. Things at the front are getting a little—shall we say, out-of-hand—and I'm afraid they get top priority as far as air cover is concerned. Half of the effective strength of this squadron is to be transferred to the front tomorrow. Both of you will be going with them. The remaining men will be told sometime this afternoon. I realise this is extremely short notice, but in war things are like that."

"Quite, sir," Jensen nodded, seemingly unmoved by the news.

Deep down inside, I felt nothing at first. Then the full significance of the other's words began to sink in. A stirring of exhilaration pervaded me. There was no doubt that things would be changed only a little at the front, instead of operating here well behind the lines, defending the cities, there would be no respite from the weariness which now seemed to be an integral part of me.

"Have you any idea of our duties, sir, once we arrive there?" I asked.

"General ground cover, with some offensive strikes against the enemy. The usual thing. You'll be flying Messerschmitts and Focke-Wulf 190s, with possibly a few Heinkels thrown in for good measure. But I've no doubt your new duties will be explained to you in much greater detail once you arrive at your destination."

"Where is that, sir?"

In answer, Graeber walked over to the large-scale map hanging on the wall of his office and jabbed at it with his finger.

"Here," he said shortly. "A small airstrip outside Bitburg. There's something brewing there, although at the moment, I don't know what it is, but from the reports which filter through occasionally, even as far back as this, it must be something big."

I followed his finger on the map, recognising the area immediately. If we were to fly as night intruders over that part of the country, we would need all of our wits about us. Heavily wooded, it was not ideal for night flying and there were too many hills in the area to make it easy even during the daytime, especially at this time of the year in middle December.

Jensen looked momentarily puzzled. He crushed out his cigarette, tilted back his chair, his eyes fixed on the map.

"I suppose that if they do intend to launch any attack against the Americans, that's one of the most logical places to do it. Not too easily defended, and a maze of roads through the forests."

Graeber smiled faintly. He said quietly: "You'll probably be called upon to keep the Allied Air Forces grounded if the weather is such that they can get into the air at all. That's where the experience of the past few weeks will come in extremely helpful."

"What you really mean sir, is that we've all learned how to fight against odds that are astronomically against us—and that we might as well die at the front as here, hitting our heads against a stone wall."

Graeber looked at Jensen for an instant, his face hard. Then the mirthless smile was back again and he nodded his head slowly. "Put it that way if you like. To be quite honest, if I had any say in the matter at all, I'd insist that you all remain here. After you're gone, the squadron will be so depleted that I doubt whether we can carry on. But our orders will be that we'll have to. Sometimes, I'm convinced that they expect miracles from us all—and there's the devil to pay if they don't get them."

"I think I undertand, sir." I looked up again as the other opened a cupboard in his desk, fished out a bottle of an amber-coloured liquid, brought out three glasses on the ends of his fingers, and placed them carefully in front of him. Methodically, he filled the glasses, waited until we had each taken one, then said slowly:

"This is the best you can get these days, I'm afraid. Nothing like the liquor you could get before the war; ersatz concoctions now, but here's to all of us, no matter what the future may hold."

"Maybe we'll meet again, someday, somewhere, sir," said Jensen, sipping his drink slowly.

Graeber shrugged. "I doubt it," he said slowly. He downed the drink in a single gulp, paused for a moment eyeing the bottle, then pushed it back into the cupboard and straightened in his chair.

Turning my head, I glanced once again at the point on

the map where the Commandant's finger had rested a few moments earlier.

The Ardennes! Now what in the name of Heaven could be brewing out there, I wondered.

CHAPTER V

Ardennes Offensive

The squadron we were leaving behind, and all of its troubles, were soon forgotten. All too soon, we were on our way by truck to the fighting zone. Now we had fresh troubles of our own to overcome, another enemy to face— an enemy far more dangerous and frightening than before, since we were on the ground, helpless, and the enemy bombers and rocket-firing Typhoons, were out over the fields and roads, shooting up every target they could find.

"We're going to be goddamned lucky if we get to the front in one piece," muttered Jensen harshly as he braced himself in the back of the swaying truck, which bounced and swayed around the sharply-angled corners in the road, the driver anxious to reach his destination before first light when the enemy planes would be out again in force and it would be virtually suicidal to be caught in the open.

What Jensen had said was a masterly understatement. We were still almost fifty miles from Bitburg and already, there was a pale greyness showing in the south-east where the dawn was beginning to brighten and with its light would come the enemy planes.

Less than a quarter of an hour to go now. I could almost sense the urgency of the situation in the way the man drove the vehicle far in excess of its permitted maximum speed. The roads were dangerous now. Knocked out vehicles and tanks still blocked them in places and detours had to be made, and in addition to this, the surface was covered with a layer of black ice, so that the tyres failed to grip properly and several times, the truck skidded and slid towards the ditch on the side of the road, threatening to overturn and spill us out into the snow-covered grass; but miraculously it remained upright and continued on into the darkness.

I buried my face in my greatcoat. I was tired, deadly tired, and in spite of myself, winced with agony, every time the truck jolted heavily to one side, throwing me against the metal struts beneath the thin canvas.

Over the tailboard of the truck, it was just possible to make out details in the growing light. Here and there, we passed the burnt-out wrecks of a line of vehicles which had been caught in the open by the enemy bombers. This was the first time I had seen such destruction at close quarters and the sight appalled me. Twisted metal and tattered canvas still showed against the greyness of the dawn. At intervals, we would pass a small group of tanks, their thick, protective hides burst and split by the terrible concussive force of the high-explosive bombs which had destroyed them.

"Sometimes, seeing this, I wish to God it was all over," muttered Hauser. He leaned forward with his elbows on his knees, resting his chin on his cupped hands. He shook his head in astonished wonder. "Why do they have to keep on fighting like this, when they must surely know that it's hopeless?"

"The same reason, I suppose, that we're going out there now, risking our lives just to prolong everything for a few more months," I said. "Orders from Berlin. There's to be no retreat. Every man has to die rather than yield up an inch of ground. It doesn't make sense, I suppose."

"If you want my opinion," interrupted Jensen harshly, "a live coward is sometimes better than a hundred dead heroes."

The truck slowed abruptly and there was the squeal of brakes as we slithered violently over the snow. Within seconds, Hauser had pulled himself savagely to his feet and was clinging to the tailboard, peering up into the grey morning sky, holding on with one hand. Swiftly, I stumbled forward as the truck lurched to a standstill and stood beside him, breathing deeply of the cold morning air. Carefully, I peered around the side of the truck, tried to make out the reason for this sudden, and unscheduled, halt.

I could see nothing. In the west, the darkness was still little short of absolute. Huge, ominous snow clouds hung close to the horizon and nothing showed up against them. "Can you see anything?"

Hausser turned, shook his head. There was a look of perplexity on his face.

"Nothing there." He paused, screwed up his eyes again, then looked back. "There's something strange going on here," he said harshly. "No obstruction on the road as far as I can see. Perfectly straight for a couple of miles. No convoy coming this way either."

"Then it must be aircraft. That's the only other explanation." I raised my head, peered up once again into the dark, cloudy sky. "Either somebody has got damned good eyesight, or a strong imagination."

"No!" Hausser yelled the warning. "There they are. I see them, coming in fast."

I twisted back, caught a fragmentary glimpse of the enemy planes as they swung in from the west. "They're circling out there," I said sharply, lowering my head and speaking to the others inside the truck. "Cloud level's barely five hundred feet. They'll have to come in low if they're to see us at all."

"They've spotted us," called Hausser. He straightened his legs, his head out of sight, hidden by the flapping canvas.

There came the sudden pounding of feet outside the truck and a second later, the breathless face of the driver looked into the back.

"Enemy aircraft, sir," he said hoarsely, glancing up at me. "They've seen us! No doubt about that, I'm afraid, nor about their intentions. We're their target, for sure."

He had run back and unlocked the tailboard before he had finished speaking. One after the other, we climbed down and stood ankle-deep in the snow, shivering for a second in the icy wind that whipped around us.

"Get under cover, away from the trucks," yelled Jensen as we stood there, hesitating. The bombers were still some distance away, circling beneath the clouds, and the danger, though ever-present, did not seem imminent. Swiftly, I galvanised myself into action. The roar of powerful engines, cutting through the frosty air, beat at my ears. Out of the corner of my eye, as I flung myself forward into the deep snow at the edge of the road, I caught a fragmentary glimpse of the planes coming in.

Fear beat up into my chest as I lay there, almost stunned by the force of my fall. Snow clung to my face and nostrils, so that my mouth opened and closed as I gasped air down into my lungs like a fish out of water. For fifteen, twenty seconds perhaps, there was nothing but the savage, ever-increasing scream of engines in my ears, blotting out everything else, so that the tired mind baulked at it, forgetting temporarily what was to follow.

While sitting in the truck, I had been comforted by the thought that perhaps the enemy had not spotted us and were looking out for bigger fish. The idea had persisted during the time I had stood helplessly watching them circle under the clouds and up to the moment when I had flung myself into the snow; but that hope had died swiftly a few seconds earlier.

Two things were suddenly clear to me as I lay there, feeling the coldness seep through my coat as the snow melted with my weight. The enemy had evidently known that some convoy would be using the road early that morning for they had clearly known where to look unless they made a habit of scouring the roads in this area every day at first light, which didn't seem likely. Secondly, there were rocket-firing Typhoons accompanying the bombers and these were the planes which our men at the front had grown to fear more than anything else; terrible weapons which could reduce a convoy to a total shambles within seconds.

The medium bombers were climbing slowly now, some half a mile away, seeking to gain the cover of a low cloud, which they would break only instants before they came in to bomb. It was the usual procedure; our own bombers had used it many times before. It gave the enemy little time in which to align their guns on them and the tremendous advantage of surprise. Against any radar-controlled fire from the ground, an attack from low level would have been suicidal. Obviously they knew that we did not possess

Such armour and that we could do little to defend ourselves against them.

Wildly, I looked about me for cover. There was nothing. The low hedge a couple of feet away afforded no protection against bullets, rockets, or bombs. A minute passed, most of the planes had moved up into the low cloud and still nothing had happened. The enemy seemed to be holding themselves in check and for one wild moment, I had the impression that they might not be going to attack us after all, that they had reconnoitred the position and decided that, being such a small convoy, we weren't worth attacking.

Twenty seconds later, the hope died instantly. The vicious, urgent thudding of a machine-gun opened up from somewhere at the head of the convoy. The first of the enemy medium bombers loomed out of the cloud less than three hundred yards away, dropping lower with every passing second.

There was scarcely time for realisation, for the first surging of fear to begin to form in my brain. It was still dark now, thick clouds forming in the east, dimming the light of the dawn. Tracers, pin-points of glowing fire, rose in a sheet to meet the diving plane, clearly seen, touching it for a second, then flicking over it as the gunner panicked, seeing the plane looming so close upon him. The tracer speared sideways, flew in a wide arc and a split second later, the gun ceased its hammering and fell silent.

The first string of bombs, black dots that were barely seen against the sky, dropped from the belly of the leading plane. My brain spun dizzily in my head for a moment, seemed to turn over once or twice, then began to function crisply and clearly again. Craning my neck, I peered directly overhead as the plane roared across my line of vision.

The plane levelled out at about four hundred feet, wisps of cloud obscuring it at intervals, the stick of bombs parallelling the planes line of flight for a brief instant, before arching lazily towards the convoy.

The first stick of bombs missed. They missed by almost twenty-five yards and crashed into the fields lining the roadway on the opposite side of the line of trucks. For those of us crouching there in the snow, the crash and concussion of the exploding bombs was terrible, ear-shattering. Great pillars of dirty snow were tossed high into the air, turbulent at their bases, streaking up into the grey sky, hanging suspended for a long, incredible moment, before falling back again, whipped a little out of shape by the keening wind.

I covered my ears with my hands, lying flat on my chest, trying to shut out the tremendous reverberations which beat through the quivering air over my head. Apart from one lone machine-gun, halfway along the convoy, there was no return fire. The second plane, coming in at a slight angle to the road, had little opposition and came in steeply, the pilot having all the time in the world in which to line up his aircraft and drop his bombs.

The approach was perfect. Little disconnected thoughts raced through my brain as I lay there and tried to make myself as small as possible in the snow. The pilots couldn't possibly see us lying there ten feet or so from the trucks, although we would stand out quite well in our dark clothing. What they were aiming for were the trucks themselves, but that thought gave me little consolation.

There was a terrible, pounding roar in my ears, shaking my entire body; a roar compounded of many things, the shriek of the falling bombs, three this time, the rocketing roar of powerful supercharged engines like a locomotive rushing through the hollowness of an endless tunnel. Each sound would have been frightening in its own right but when taken together, blended into something indefinably terrifying, they brought a feeling of suffocating horror into the base of my throat, so that I found it almost impossible to breathe.

Jensen was yelling something at the top of his voice, but the words were indistinguishable above the shrieking roar and I turned my head away. Oh God, this must surely be the end of us. The enemy couldn't possibly miss every time, not under such perfect bombing conditions as these, not having to bother about anti-aircraft fire or interference from our own planes. There was no chance of getting away from them. The pilots knew their job well and intended carrying it out to the bitter end, remaining until they had destroyed us utterly and completely.

For a fraction of a second, the bombs hung suspended in the sky as if held by invisible wires, before being allowed to continue their fall. Then, abruptly, they speared downwards and struck. The first landed some ten feet in front of the first truck in the convoy, the second and third falling directly among the trucks.

There was no time to crawl away, no time to think or even to hope. The bombs exploded with a cavernous roar of flame and shuddering concussion. Something beat at the side of my body like the slap of a gigantic fist, pushing me over on one side. The earth erupted into reaching columns of dirt. One of the trucks flew upwards in a dozen twisted pieces that came crashing down again into the middle of the roadway, splintering and crumpling as they hit.

Somewhere, a man screamed thinly in mortal agony, the tiny wail being lost instantly in the beating thunder of the plane, following closely on the heels of the second. I held my breath, was aware of the sick fear in my body and the dull pounding of blood in my temples. With an effort, I lifted my head, gulped down a breath of smoke-filled air, almost gagged on it as it burned my lungs.

One of the trucks, some thirty yards away was on fire, blazing furiously, petrol from the ruptured tank flowing across the road, melting the snow in its path as the licking tongues of flame, eating their way hungrily along it, burst up in all directions. I saw one of the men lying in the ditch suddenly leap to his feet as the stream of fire raced across his body.

His clothing alight, he ran out, screaming, into the middle of the roadway, his arms flailing wildly above his head. The flames, fanned by the wind and his own movement, licked fiercely about him, leaping up around his shoulders and head as two other men ran forward in an attempt to catch him.

For a second, the man's thin, high-pitched shriek of fear rose thin and clear above the thunder of the fourth plane coming in from the east, died abruptly as the two men caught him and threw him down onto the slippery surface of the icy road. They slid for several yards across the surface, then came to rest in the snow on the far side of the road. Savagely, the men beat at the flames with their bare hands, disregarding the planes still coming in on their bombing runs.

More bombs fell in a cluster, blotting out the trio of men in the middle of the road. Something black and jagged seemed to spin out of the air towards me, crashing against my forehead. There was a searing pain lancing into my brain and for a moment, I must have lost consciousness because the first sensation I had was of pain in my right leg and of the sharp crackling of flames in the near distance. With a quick, desperate heave, I pushed myself up onto my elbows, shook my head to clear it of the mists which seemed to be fogging it, and glanced about me through eyes which were brimming with tears.

Numbly, I forced my eyes to remain open. Most of the trucks seemed to be enveloped in flame, black oily smoke mingling with the dust which still hung in the air. Slowly, some of the terrible numbness began to go away. I sucked in a deep breath, then fell back again as the pain welled up inside me again.

Something streaked across my stultified vision, hammered into the roadway at the front of the column of trucks. The salvo of rockets were dead on their target. The trucks had been set on fire by the bombs and the rockets now completed the task of destruction. Nothing was left of the first two vehicles as the Typhoon roared overhead and began to climb steeply into the clouds.

My feet and fingers slipped on the ice underneath the snow as I tried desperately to pull myself forward, away from the trucks which were now death-traps instead of the protection they had earlier promised. There was no escape from those dreadful rockets. Terribly accurate, swift and straight, they lanced down on trails of fire and smoke, exploding in channels along the sides of the road, picking out their targets in erupting curtains of flame.

The very tissue of the air was torn and split asunder by the onslaught of those explosive charges, not as loud as the bombs, but with a continuing roar that went on and on and on.

Incredibly, this was the last attack upon the convoy.

The last of the Typhoons roared away into the distance, vanishing into the clouds and I picked myself up slowly, feeling the warm slickness of blood on the side of my head, running down my cheeks. The snow, where I had lain a few moments earlier, was stained with red and I put up my hand experimentally, looked down at the blood on the glove with a feeling akin to surprise, then wiped them on my tunic.

I stood for a long moment, swaying precariously, then reached out with my hand towards the side of the truck nearby. Gingerly, I tried to move my limbs, was surprised to find that no bones had been broken. Several of the trucks were on fire and blazing fiercely. The men with the extinguishers were in action within seconds of the departure of the planes.

Indeed, if anything was to be saved, they had to be in action instantly. Water would have spread a petrol fire, increased the area of conflagration and it was essential to confine it as far as possible. There was no sign of the man who had been on fire, or of his two companions who had attempted so desperately to beat out the flames. I glanced around for them for a long moment, then paused as my gaze fell on the large, wrinkle-edged crater in the middle of the road at almost the precise point where they had been lying, flat on their faces, just as the last bomber had come roaring in.

The picture told its story. They could never have survived that direct hit and the only good thing was that they had doubtless died instantly. The foam extinguishers were of only limited capacity, but most of the petrol fires seemed to have been got under control by the time the rest of the men had attacked the flames, using the only water available to them, the snow which lay around us in profusion. A group of men were shovelling it onto the flames with an almost frantic speed and gradually they were getting the fires under complete control.

Seven of the ten trucks in the convoy had been completely destroyed, were total wrecks which would never move again, and three men had been caught in them, killed by the blast and shrieking shrapnel before they had had time to scramble clear. Two men clambered among the still smouldering wrecks and pulled them out, charred remains which were no longer recognisable as human beings.

I knew I had to pull myself together, that it was essential to keep my head. It must have been terrible for those men, trapped in the bombed and blazing trucks, unable to get out while the flames beat and scorched around them, burning through clothing and flesh, through bones and sinews . . .

The thought almost broke me in half and shuddering, I turned away. I felt sick and was afraid that I would throw up in an instant, the moment I walked forward, but the knowledge that there might be more men trapped in those wrecked trucks, drove me on, overriding all other emotions and fears. Gradually, the sickness went away and a cold anger and determination took its place. The smoke was thinning slowly, the dust beginning to settle. Never had devastation been so thorough or so complete.

The entire area, the whole stretch of the road had been turned into a quagmire of mud and melting snow, gaping craters and shattered vehicles. Two of the trucks, those immediately in front of that in which we had been travelling, had been completely wrecked, the bent and twisted remains, blackened and charred, lying on their sides. Slowly, I walked along the column. Fires were still burning here and there and steam rose in choking clouds where shovelfuls of snow had been piled onto the red-hot axles and chassis.

At the head of the column, the lone machine-gun which had opened up at the approach of the planes, lay on its side, twisted and bent as though smashed by a heavy blow. The gunner lay beside it, his eyes staring sightlessly into the brightening heavens, his lips drawn back in a grimace of surprised horror. There was a line of small holes across his chest which had not bled much, but there was no doubt that he had died instantly, still facing the diving enemy.

"Poor devil," muttered Jensen softly. "He never knew what him him."

I smiled faintly. "We're all in the same boat. We must have lost nearly half of the men."

"Let's get back along the column and check on the casualties," said the other heavily. "No chance of a miracle, I suppose."

"None at all judging by the damage."

Ten minutes later, we knew the worst. The remaining three trucks were still serviceable and in running order, although it would still be difficult to manoeuvre them around those which had been knocked out and there seemed little chance of making a detour. Two of our pilots had been killed and one, Schmidt, was badly wounded. The others had, miraculously, escaped injury, but over a dozen of the troops who had been accompanying us, had died in the attack and more than twice that number had been injured.

I shivered in a sudden flurry of sleet, then bent forward, head well down against the wind, pushing my way forward.

"We'll get moving as soon as possible, even with the three trucks we've got left. There's no telling how far we can get with them in their present condition." He spoke absently, suddenly an old and defeated man; Jensen, the man I never thought I would see so dejected. "Things may get a little more difficult now. They'll throw in everything they've got before midday."

"We've met them before," I conceded.

"Fifty-fifty on our chances," he said harshly. "No more than that; and that's probably overstating them a little." He seemed to be talking to himself.

Even as we stood there, a group of tanks rumbled by, the drivers sticking their heads through the turrets, surveying the damage, a look of incredulity on their rugged features. One of them shook his head unbelievingly.

"You know, maybe Graeber was right when he said there was something brewing in this area," I said sharply.

Jensen raised his head, looked at me for a moment, then nodded. "Something big, he said. Maybe he *was* right. These tanks aren't moving up here for nothing." There was a look of astonished surprise on his face as he went on quickly: "You don't think there is going to be an attack on the American lines, do you?"

"Could be. If there is, we're going to find ourselves

in the thick of it before we know where we are."

Wearily, we clambered back into the truck, settled ourselves on the hard wooden boards. A moment later, the engine was started up again and we moved off with a violent jerk that almost threw me off my seat.

What a set-up, I thought savagely, what a stupid, goddamned set-up. The enemy seemed to hold undisputed sway over the air. So far, we had seen nothing of our planes and more defeat rolled over me as I sat there, feeling the bitterness in my mouth.

The enemy must surely know that we were moving up to the front. The planes held the key to the game which was being played on this area. Our only hope was that the weather would break completely, that fog or low cloud would shroud the area and allow us to move up our troops and armour under its cover.

CHAPTER VI

Tank Busters

I remembered very little of that nightmare journey through the winter countryside to Bitburg. Some time after leaving the scene of carnage on that lonely road, I must have fallen asleep in the jolting, swaying truck, the after-effects of that terrible period of bombing still affecting my brain. My head spun like a kite in a high wind and I felt physically and mentally tired and sick.

The route was filled with detours, roadblocks and bomb craters and it was early afternoon before we had covered the fifty or so miles to Bitburg. Driving through the town, I was struck by the absence of bomb damage and the vast number of tanks and armoured vehicles in sight. The entire place was one, huge arsenal, I realised. Troops were embarking in lorries, preparing to move out to the west and there seemed to be the best part of three battalions there.

There was a foul, bitter taste in my mouth and I sat

up slowly. We seemed to have taken a great many turnings during the journey and I had lost all sense of direction by the time my mind came back to normal. Tenderly, I massaged the muscles at the back of my neck. There was a dull ache suffused through my body and a pain in my shoulders and arms where they were pressed against the side of the truck.

Leaving the town of Bitburg, we drove slowly along narrow winding roads, then turned into a wide opening, beyond which lay a perimeter track and a couple of runways crossing at a slight angle. As an airfield, it had nothing to recommend it. There was a handful of planes standing in front of the single hangar, and a crash tender standing on the opposite side of the airfield, on the perimeter track.

One of the smallest airfields I had even seen; which was probably the main reason why the enemy had left it alone, why it had not been bombed out of commission earlier. Situated so close behind the front line, it must have been one of the few airfields still operational.

We halted in front of the row of Nissen huts, tucked away among the trees.

"So this is our new home," muttered Hausser as we climbed down and stood surveying the scene. "We finally made it."

"The weather doesn't look too good. From the flying point of view, I mean."

Jensen nodded, threw a quick glance at the sky. "There's a big change coming—and soon. It's getting warmer. That means fog unless I'm very much mistaken."

"Fog." I stared at him. The air was still cold and it seemed impossible that he could have detected any change in the temperature.

"I reckon so. In fact, I'm pretty certain. I've seen this abrupt change in the weather before."

"Then there'll be no flying for us for some time," muttered Hausser. "I'm beginning to feel glad that we came here. *Himmel*, but I could do with a couple of nights uninterrupted sleep. I'd give anything for that. Afterwards, I'll take anything that comes."

Suddenly, surprisingly, Jensen smiled briefly. He sighed.

"Remember the troops at the front. If they intend to start an attack, they'll be needing all the air support they can get. We may have to fly, good weather or bad. Fog or not."

"That's what I was afraid of," Hausser nodded. Our footstep crunched in unison as we walked towards the empty Nisson huts. Under normal circumstances, we would have reported to the Commandant right away, intimated our presence on the airfield. But that would come later. There had been little or no rest possible on the journey from Kassel and all the men were bone-weary. Rest was essential, vital, if they were to play their part.

* * * *

From the relative warmth of the Nissen hut, I stood by the window and looked out at the cloud-flecked sky outside. It was still bitterly cold, but there was no longer any sign of frost, the temperature was about ten degrees above freezing and the snow here, which had been very thin, had disappeared almost entirely and there was only mud, a thick, gluey mud which covered everything and would turn the roads and fields in the area into a quagmire by early morning if the temperature continued to rise.

There would be little chance for tanks in the forthcoming battle and the infantry, if they went in at all and the attack was not postponed, would be forced to slog their way forward against stiffening enemy opposition.

I supposed I ought to have felt bitter about the powers which had ordered us there, with their belief in the supremacy of Germany even in the face of the inescapable facts, with their wall charts and maps and little pins stuck in them, shuffling men and machines around like pawns on a chessboard. But the thought died almost unborn. It was, I knew, possibly unjust. One had to believe in something; and if not in Germany, then in what?

I supposed too, that I ought to have felt cynical, ironic and angry, at the sight of the battered planes outside, just visible in the light of dawn. But curiously enough, I couldn't. I knew what these planes were capable of;

we could ask nothing more of them.

"Wonder what the new Commandant will say when he meets us for the first time?" muttered Hausser.

"No idea," I said, shrugging. "I'm curious to see what his attitude is going to be towards us, how he's going to handle it. The situation will be somewhat confused." He smiled, but the smile did not travel as far as his eyes. "Not to mention the fact that, as you predicted, the weather has closed down almost completely."

"We'll soon find out," muttered Jensen absently. He glanced over my shoulder to where the mist was hanging low over the fields and the woods in the distance, some quarter of a mile away which we had noticed yesterday, were completely invisible.

Somewhere in the distance, low on the horizon, there was a faint, but continuous, rumble. A sound which I had heard many times before, knowing instinctively what it was. Heavy artillery fire. And there was another sound, fainter, becoming louder at irregular intervals, a moaning sigh high up above the thickening clouds.

The field commanders were evidently playing it safe. A tremendous barrage of V.1s going over, possibly directly aimed at the enemy-held ports. Our turn would come later, I thought, once the attack had gained momentum. There seemed little doubt that the enemy would be taken by surprise.

From what little I had been able to learn during the past few hours since arriving at the small airfield, the Americans although present in strength on either side of the wide front, to the north and south; were extremely thin on the ground in the centre. That was where the main brunt of our attack was due to fall had perhaps fallen.

Twenty minutes later, I made my way to the Commandant's office in one of the Nissen huts close to the concrete Control Block. Helmann, the Commandant, was a tall, thin-faced man, who held himself very straight as he stood behind his desk and eyed me speculatively. I screwed up my eyes in automatic reflex as I entered to adjust them to the gloom inside the hut. There was a log fire burning in a stove at the far end, but it gave off little warmth and water was dripping through a split in the iron roof. The furniture consisted of the polished wooden desk and three plain chairs with a single map of the combat area on the wall.

I had a brief impression of hardness in the other's face and an inquiring lift of his pale eyebrows. His eyes were grey with an ironic glint. There was not so much a marked hostility in his glance as a lack of interest. He looked a tired and defeated man in spite of his military bearing.

"As you're new here, I think I ought to explain the situation to you as I see it. You may have guessed that there's something big happening here. The American forces are all deployed for attack on this front. North of the Ardennes, he has some sixteen divisions and to the south, there are, according to our latest information, ten divisions. But here, on the central sector, there are only five facing us and of these, most of the American troops are untried. This is where we have struck, and we intend to drive a wide corridor through their front and head for the Meuse."

I eyed him speculatively. "And just where do we come in, sir?"

"That's simple. You've only got to take one look at the country out here to know how this battle will have to be fought. It's rolling, forested country broken by the steep and twisted valleys of numerous mountain streams. Plenty of roads, but very few of them in good condition, particularly at this time of the year. Most of them have to pass through narrow and awkward defiles where the enemy's armour will find it exceedingly difficult to manoeuvre. We'll hit them hard and we'll hit them fast. Surprise has been complete acording to the reports I've received.

"Most of the tactical advantage has been created by the V.1s sent over during the early hours of the morning. Now that we've achieved surprise, it is time for the Luftwaffe to step in and help our forward troops."

"What's the weather like over the fighting zone, sir?"

"You'll get the latest information from the Meteorological Section. So far as I know, the cloud base is less than three hundred feet and lowering rapidly. There seems to be little chance of it improving too, in the foreseeable future."

"And you expect us to go out in that, sir?"

"Naturally. Those are your orders." The Commandant looked at me in mild surprise, then shrugged. "If you're afraid, of course, I can always—" He left the remainder of his sentence unsaid, but the meaning behind it was obvious, painfully so.

"I'm not afraid," I said stiffly, "and you know it. The same goes for the rest of the pilots. We've been flying in weather far worse than this back there at Kassel."

"All right. All right." The twist of Helmann's eyebrows robbed the words of any menace. "But from now on, you'll have to fly around the clock if this attack is to gain the momentum it must have to drive it all the way through to the Meuse. The R.A.F. and U.S.A.A.F. have been grounded most of the night and morning. The weather back there, behind their lines, must be even worse than here. But they'll come out in their hundreds as soon as the mist clears, we can rely on that. It's your job to stop them, but more than that, you have another task to perform."

"I'm afraid I don't quite understand, sir? Another job?"

He nodded. "Exactly. They'll be moving up tanks and troops to the front as soon as things settle down and the element of surprise wears off. You'll have to destroy them before they get here."

"Tank busters."

"That's right. You catch on quick. I'll admit that these planes aren't ideal for the job, but they're the best we have. We can fit them up with temporary bomb racks if necessary, but mostly, we'll need you to shoot up their convoys while they're still on the road.

"Germany is not finished yet, as the Americans and British will soon find out to their cost. The tide of the war is turning slowly but surely in our favour. Germany will rise again. The Feuhrer is confident, and I'm sure of it."

"The Feuhrer."

"Exactly. The orders for the attack have come directly

from him. They have to be carried out to the letter."

"I can quite believe that," I said bitterly. "Have you told all this to the others?"

"Most of them." Helmann went back to his desk and lowered himself stiffly into his chair. His face seemed more angular, sharper than before. He sucked in his cheeks reflectively, rapping idly with his fingers. For a moment, he seemed to have forgotten my presence there, then he shook his head slightly and looked straight at me.

"That's all for the moment," he said quietly. I turned away, then paused with my hand on the handle of the door as he said thinly: "Just one thing I want to make clear. I know exactly how things will be in the future around here. I know what you and your men will be going through, because unlike most Commandant's, I too, was a fighter pilot until three months ago.

"I know men perhaps a little more than you realise. Every man is what his environment and heredity make him. Nothing more and nothing less. I don't expect impossibilities or miracles, because I don't believe in them. All I ask is that every man does his best."

"Yes, sir." I went outside and closed the door gently behind me. On the airfield, the ground crews were already checking the planes, refuelling them, moving up the belts of ammunition for the wing cannon.

The day was raw and wet, unbelievably wet, unless you knew what it could be like in December in the Ardennes. By two o'clock, the planes were ready for take-off. The wind had dropped almost to zero but the mist was still hanging over the trees and fields. Visibility was down to less than a hundred yards and I had no doubt that it would drop still further by nightfall.

Heaving my chute into the cockpit, I stood by the wing of the fighter and looked about me. The rest of the pilots were climbing on board their machines, checking their 'chutes and equipment. They were moving fast. Good men, I thought, who would give of their best as the Commandant demanded. But sooner or later, they would crack. It was inevitable.

I gave them one last thought, then turned my attention

to the plane. Carefully, I swung myself into the cockpit, checked the instruments.

Here in the cockpit, everything was instantly familiar. The faint smell of high octane fuel mingled with other, indefinable odours and chemical smells that touched my nostrils and tingled at the back of my throat. I glanced out through the canopy. There was the old. familiar fear lancing through my body and the strange tightening sensation in my legs which never went away. With an effort, I shrugged the sensation off. I had faced this before, and I would face it again. But there always seemed to be that peculiar moment of commitment when the feeling of strained tension took a hold on my body, knotting the muscles of my stomach into a jangled ball of nerves.

It was not exactly fear, but something akin to it. Looking back on things, I could remember the same kind of signs in Hausser and Jensen and the others, the taut, electric feeling that you were walking out into the middle of a huge stage, that you and no one else, were playing the star part and the most interested spectator in the audience was—death.

The drizzle was marking the side of the canopy as I started up the engine, heard the spluttering cough which always came before full power. Then the propeller turned, slowly at first, but gathering momentum until it was a glittering, transparent blur that was more imagined than actually seen.

I ran the engine up for several seconds, going through the routine pre-flight checks which had been a part of me for so long. After a while, they had become automatic and there was little need to think about them. A couple of minutes later, the engine was warm enough for take-off. The chocks were pulled away from beneath the wheels and I taxied slowly around the perimeter track towards the end of the runway. Two of the planes were already there, one was halfway along the runway, wheels lifting smoothly from the ground.

While I waited for take-off, I throttled back the engine and went through the cockpit check once more, just to be on the safe side. There was no point in taking unnecessary chances at this stage of the proceedings.

The plane immediately in front of me began to move down the stretching concrete river of the runway, accelerating as it moved away. Everything was ready for take-off. A calm and distant voice in my headphones gave me the order to go.

The wet grey afternoon sky lay stretched out in front of me as I eased power into the engine, felt the aircraft throb and vibrate as I steered the plane with the throttles.

Slowly, the engine came up to full power as I rumbled forward. The plane's speed increased sharply, the concrete of the runway rumbled beneath the wheels, flashing by in a blur of grey as the aircraft began its rapid, uneven motion, gathering velocity swiftly now. The engine roared. Gently, I eased back on the stick, took the pressure off the nose and checked the airspeed indicator once more.

Everything was reacting normally. One of the markers along the edge of the runway slipped past and a second later, I felt the sudden change in the vibration as the plane became airborne. Flipping up the gear handle, I waited until I heard the undercarriage click into place with a softly muffled metallic sound.

Circling, I climbed to a thousand feet and almost instantly found myself in the dense cloud. It closed on in about me like a stretching mass of grey cotton-wool; visibility dropped virtually to zero. Clamping a tight grip on my mind I concentrated on the instruments. There was always an element of danger associated with taking off in weather like this. These grey cumulus clouds were full of fighters taking off and circling the airfield, climbing to their pre-arranged height. It took only one pilot to panic, one man to distrust his instruments and try to get out of the clouds by the shortest possible route, climbing to a height which had not been scheduled for him, and there could be one of the biggest air crashes known.

The only comfort in my mind was that all of these men were experienced pilots. They knew that to trust their instruments implicitly and to disregard their natural instincts was the only way to stay alive.

I kept my gaze fixed on the instrument panel, checking height and airspeed automatically. There was no point in trying to check my position by anything outside, there was nothing to see but a wet greyness that wrapped the plane around until it seemed to be held motionless in the grip of something gigantic. Settling myself more comfortably in my seat, I sat patiently until the cloud began to thin. Tattered wisps of it moved past the cockpit, flowing over the plane like smoke. Then, three minutes later, still flying according to the pattern, I broke free of the cloud altogether and came out into the brilliantly clear air at five thousand feet. Below me, there was a sea of greyness that stretched unbroken from horizon to horizon in every conceivable direction. I could see nothing of ground details, but a moment later, glancing about me, I spotted the rest of the flight, some a couple of hundred feet above me, the rest climbing up out of the cloud.

"Everybody on course now?" Jensen's voice came over the intercom, sounding tinny and far-away.

"On course, oh-nine-seven degrees," I said automatically.

The others gave confirmation a moment later and we formed up into tight formation. On the instrument panel, the A.S.I. had moved further over and now stood at almost three hundred miles per hour. The airfield was lost somewhere beneath the cloud behind us. For the next twenty minutes, at least, we would be flying over friendly territory, and there would not be any action until we crossed the front line and dropped down below the cloud.

Craning my neck, I glanced over the metal lip of the canopy, looked down below me. Everywhere, lay that dripping grey blanket of cloud, blotting out all view of the ground.

"It's going to be a devil of a job getting down below that cloud base," said a voice suddenly, which I recognised after an instant as belonging to Albrecht. "Less than five hundred feet and probably lowering rapidly if the experts can be relied upon to give us a correct picture."

"All the more reason for us to go through with this attack," said Jensen slowly. He seemed to be choosing his words carefully. "We'll be out of the cloud and shooting them up before they know where we are."

"They'll still be able to hear us, even above the cloud," I pointed out.

"That's true." The other's voice was calm and un-hurried. "But even so, we've got the advantage of tactical surprise and that will count for a lot in this kind of attack."

We flew in silence for several minutes. Down below there was no sign of any breaks in the overall cloud cover. It seemed to blot out everything. We were alone in a clear, almost frosty world utterly divorced from the ground below. No longer did we belong to the earth; we were creatures of the air, the vast, open spaces above the clouds where the sun, although wintry, shone brilliantly. Very soon, the air inside the cockpit was comfortably warm.

"Nearly there," said Jensen suddenly. "Check every-thing. We don't want any mistakes once we go in."

"Still no sign of any breaks in that cloud," muttered Eberbach. "We'll be flying blind for most of the way. Let's hope there aren't any hills in this area. At this speed, by the time we break out of the cloud cover, we won't have a chance in hell if there's anything in the way."

"That's a risk we've got to take," said Jensen savagely.

Silence fell again. Inwardly, I knew what each man was thinking, sitting there behind the controls of the throbbing, vibrating planes, engrossed in his own thoughts, wondering what might lie under that blanket of cloud, what hidden dangers there might be down there, waiting to trap the unwary. The pulse rate was already quickening to meet the unknown.

Inside two minutes, we had crossed the forward lines of the armies on the ground. Occasionally, where the cloud thinned, but did not actually break, it was possible to make out a vivid flash as something exploded on the ground, but these were diffuse things, not sharply-defined details which might have been of immense help to us.

"We'll go down in line astern," said Jensen sharply. "I want everyone to keep their eyes peeled for any obstruc-tions there might be once we break cloud. Take whatever evasive action may be necessary. This is going to be tricky."

Out of the corner of my eye, I saw his plane tilt over on one wing-tip, then go down steeply, diving towards the clouds. It vanished from sight into the eternal greyness a split second before I threw over the stick to follow him. The sunlight dimmed, then was blotted out of existence as the cloud swallowed me up. The pleasant sensation of warmth, vanishing in an instant, brought only a damp coldness in its wake. I shivered uncontrollably for a moment, then hunched forward in my seat and tried to relax, to ignore the feeling of almost unbearable tension that was building up inside my chest. The bleak, chill greyness seemed to continue all the way to the ground.

There was nothing on which I could check my position. Jensen's plane was lost to view. Behind me, there would be other aircraft diving on my tail and I could see nothing of them either. I was all alone in a bleak, wet world, unable to see anything, knowing only that the ground was down there somewhere, rushing up to meet me, and that unless I was very lucky, I would hit it before the cloud cleared, before I was even aware of its presence.

For an instant, the cloud thinned. The altimeter showed a little over two thousand feet. I had a brief, fragmentary glimpse of the ground beneath me, then the scene was swallowed up again as the cloud thickened once more and I could see nothing. But that brief glimpse had been sufficient to show me that there, directly below us, the ground was flat but heavily wooded and there had been a road stretching diagonally across my line of vision.

Outside the cockpit, the drizzle was running in streams off the transparent plastic. Below us, somewhere along that maze of winding, twisting road, the enemy would be moving up their guns and tanks and troops, striving to maintain his balance in the face of this sudden, and totally unexpected attack. It had been a master stroke on our part, I reflected, to beat the Americans to the punch and in the one sector where we stood any chance of success. If only we could gain sufficient momentum while the enemy were reeling back in shocked surprise, nothing could stop us. The Americans would undoubtedly have huge ammunition dumps and stocks of precious petrol set up somewhere behind their lines. Once we had those in our possession things would be a lot easier.

Our task was to destroy any reinforcements they might be rushing up to the front; the only problem left now, would be to find them.

This was a vast area and the twisting roads, overhung by the heavily-forested patches, offered sanctuary for their truck and tank drivers. It would be extremely difficult to pick them out from the air, especially at this speed and with the cloud base so low. We would possibly have a minute at the most in which to scour the entire area, before having to climb back into the clouds again.

During that time, we would have to make as complete a survey of the immediate terrain as possible, take note of any American convoys there might be on the roads, and also keep an eye open for any gun emplacements which might make things disagreeable for us on the main run in.

But if the twisting roads offered cover for the enemy troop convoys, they were also a deadly trap. In places, high, rock-strewn hills bordered them and one slip, a sharp turn by a panic-stricken driver, and the truck would lurch off the road, down the steep, precipitous side of a hundred-foot ravine.

All of these thoughts flashed through my mind in the brief seconds before I broke cloud. In that same instant, Jensen said sharply, uregently: "Everything is pretty level. No hills in sight, no convoys either, I'm afraid."

Levelling out at a little under five hundred feet, I gave the engine minimum throttle, feeding them the maximum weak mixture so that I might conserve as much fuel as possible for the return flight.

"It's uncannily quiet down there," said Eberbach in a hushed whisper. "Nothing moving as far as I can see."

"There's got to be something somewhere around." Jensen's voice was harsh and urgent. "Keep a sharp look-out."

I dropped lower. The roads were narrow strips of grey that stood out starkly against the overall greenness of the wooded areas. I tried looking at things with averted vision. Finally, it paid off.

Something moved slowly, almost imperceptibly at the edge of my gaze and I swung my head sharply to follow it. In a flash I spotted them again, turned the plane in a wide circle.

"Something down there," I said briefly. "Looks like

tanks moving up. Ten, maybe twenty of them. Some armoured trucks."

"I see them too," called Hausser. "That looks some size of a convoy."

"Any sign of guns in the area?" Jensen spoke coolly and briskly.

Ten seconds passed, ten seconds in which we followed each other in line astern, diving down out of the clouds towards the tank convoy that made its way slowly forward along the twisting road. Every second, I expected to see the rippling red splashes of gunfire rising up from the enemy trucks which accompanied the tanks, but there was nothing. It was as if they were so sure that the only planes in the area would be their own, that they had never paused to consider the possibility that we might be attacking them.

Then someone in the convoy must have woken to the fact that we were the enemy. Two of the leading trucks immediately accelerated, pulled away from the rest of the convoy, reached a sharp-angled bend in the road and halted there, swinging round so as to almost block the road.

Then there was little time in which to take notice of them. I put the nose of the plane down, heard the sound of the engine rise in pitch above the thin screaming of the air around the canopy.

CHAPTER VII

Wings Over The Ardennes

Immediately, the tension grew. My eyes were fixed intently on the line of grey shapes which had halted on the road as though aware that there was no chance of escape, that to try to run for cover would have been madness. I felt my eyes blink over the wide-open stare, then peered through the sights at the tanks, turning the plane slightly to line it up on the road. In front of me, Jensen's plane was a dark, flashing shape, arrowing downwards, just visible against the variegated background which acted as an excellent camouflage.

The enemy tanks were strung out at precise, mathematical intervals along the road, keeping well in to the side so as not to block it for traffic coming in the opposite direction. I barely had time to notice that several of them had elevated their turret guns and were trying to take desperate aim at us, when I was almost over the top of the convoy. Savagely, with a faint feeling of exultation, I pressed the firing button. Even above the shrieking roar of the engine, it was possible to hear the shuddering, rasping echoes of the guns as they beat their staccato rattle of hatred along the wings.

The lines of tracer speared down towards the tanks and armoured cars, converging on them as though drawn magically together. The shells splashed against the thick armour of the tanks as I held my hand against the firing button, lifting the nose of the plane slightly, levelling out. Swiftly, the fire passed over the whole length of the convoy, missing nothing.

As far as the tanks were concerned, the shells seemed to have little effect on the thick armour, but the trucks near the end of the convoy were a different matter. There was a sudden blinding flash that erupted with a shocking abruptness from the last truck but one. Black smoke boiled up into the air, thrown high by the tremendous force of the explosion. Bits of wreckage flew through the air around me as I lived through the smoke, then pulled clear.

"What the devil was that?" Jensen's voice ran in my ears.

I levelled out just below the clouds and flicked on the switch of the intercom. "Must have been an ammunition truck," I said hoarsely. "Nothing else could have exploded like that. Probably the tracer that did it."

"Whatever it was, that's one lot of ammunition they won't be getting up to the front. We'll go in again. Strafe the tanks too, although this cannon fire doesn't seem to be having much effect."

"We need bombs if we're to do anything about them," I said thickly. "After all, they can't expect a cannon shell to penetrate a couple of inches of hardened steel."

"Maybe they figure we ought to be going low enough to shoot through the vizors," interrupted Eberbach. He seemed to be smiling to himself.

"If you care to try it, go ahead." Jensen's voice was unnaturally sharp.

"Just an idea."

"Sure. And those are the kind of ideas that could lose us men and planes." Jensen couldn't keep the cynicism out of his voice.

We turned in a wide circle, keeping below the cloud. Apart from the trucks drawn up at either end of the convoy, there did not seem likely to be any serious opposition. A fighter pilot's paradise, I thought wearily, if only the cloud base had been a little higher and the rain had ceased allowing us to see clearly.

This time, we were even luckier than the first. By the time we had climbed over the end of the convoy, all of the trucks at the rear had been destroyed utterly or set on fire. Of the vehicle which had been carrying the ammunition, nothing remained. It was as if it had never existed. Two tanks had also been destroyed by lucky hits and the road had been blocked completely as four of the tanks in the centre of the convoy had tried to turn and run for it.

Several troops had been spotted lying by the side of the road and the sight of them had brought a memory stirring into my mind, of the time when the positions had been reversed, and I had lain there, waiting for the bombs and rockets to blow me to pieces. There was still a lingering sensation of savage exultation and exhilaration in my body as I climbed up into the clouds, aware of the others around me even though I could not see them.

The end of the convoy had been swift and curiously unspectacular. There had been few violent explosions. Smoke had poured from several of the vehicles as the cannon shells had hit the fuel tanks or the stocks of petrol which were being carried up to the front.

We formed up again at six thousand feet, turned on the course which would take us back to the airfield. The sun was already dropping down towards the west and the short winter afternoon was almost over. Very soon, it would be dark.

"The cloud's beginning to break a little directly ahead."

Albrecht's voice sounded suddenly on the intercom. I lifted my head instinctively, searched the dimness ahead with tired eyes and could see nothing for a long moment. Then, as if by magic, the clouds cleared beneath us. It was possible to see the ground, misty and vague, it was true, but it was the ground.

Down there, it was almost dusk. Greens and browns and greys were all blended together into a vast and stretching panorama which lay spread out under us like some magic carpet. It was a wonderful and beautiful scene; quiet and peaceful with nothing to show that guns were firing, shells were exploding, and men were dying down there at that very instant.

Quite suddenly, the war seemed very far away. For a moment, there was nothing but the quietness and stillness such as I had known many times before the war, in the unhurried, balmy days of the early thirties. With an effort, I shook the feeling of unreality away. That was the dream which had existed long ago. It had no part in the world today.

Out of the corner of my eye, I glimpsed the sprinkling of tiny lights, the brilliant white flashes that showed up briefly on the ground over on the starboard bow.

"Tracer," said Jensen, as though divining my thoughts. "Looks as though there's a battle going on down there right this minute."

I nodded to myself. This was the reality, I thought bitterly. There was death in all of its glory, there was fear and destruction. Men lying dead or wounded in the hedgerows or in the grass of the fields. Guns hurling their wrath at the enemy, shells blowing themselves apart in a hail of jagged splinters that tore through a man's body in an instant of red-edged time.

With an effort, I repressed the shudder that ran through me and thought about the men in the squadron who had come out here with Jensen and myself. These were the times when a man stood out on his own merit, was recognised for what he was. The testing time for everyone.

For most of the men, who had lived through the terrible night and day attacks at Kassel, who body and mind had been scourged by the snow and the terrible weariness, things could never be the same again. For some men, such as Jensen himself, and possibly Hausser, the weariness had little meaning. Always, they seemed wide-awake and alert, seemingly indestructible, taking everything as it came, ignoring the trivial things and concentrating only on those things which really mattered in the long run. For them, flying was the only thing that mattered. They lived for it and for Germany, and one day, I thought bitterly, they would die for them.

There were other men, exemplified by Eberbach and Albrecht, who were utterly weary beyond words, but who somehow managed to find the strength to keep on going, when every instinct must have told them that it was useless and that the only sensible thing to do was to let go, to surrender the body to the exquisite and infinite weariness which threatened to overwhelm it, and grew worse and more unendurable every day.

And somewhere in between these types of men, were the vast majority such as myself. By now, we had gone past the point of caring what was happening to us, no longer were we afraid of the enemy as such. There was no fear of the enemy. We knew him now and we did not fear him. We had seen too much of death and destruction for it to have any further effect on us.

That was something in the past. By now, we had grown used to looking only one day ahead at a time. Anything beyond that had no real meaning as far as we were concerned.

Thirty minutes later, we arrived back over the airfield. The wind had risen slightly and the cloud base was higher now, contrary to the information we had been given by the Meteorological experts before taking off. Below a thousand feet it was reasonably clear and the rain had stopped.

Wings level and steady, nose down, I went in to land. Undercarriage down, I lined up on the runway in use, checked the flaps because of the strong wind which was blowing hard from starboard, and throttled back. The plane touched down with a bump and a bleating protest of tortured rubber as the tyres hit the rough surface of the runway. For a second, it threatened to go into a spin, then righted itself and I rolled to a near standstill at the far end of the runway, turning with the throttle, easing the plane gently around the perimeter track, to come to a final halt in front of the solitary hangar.

As I switched off the engine, I felt my body surrender itself to the dragging fatigue which I had been fighting against consciously all the way back. There had been so many things on my mind during the flight that it was only now, when all immediate danger was past, that reaction was beginning to set in.

For a long moment, my body seemed incapable of movement. I sat in the confined space of the cockpit, aware that the two members of the ground crew had come forward, were fussing around the plane, checking superficially for damage, going over every inch, making notes of shell holes which would have to be plugged up before the next flight.

My brain felt exhausted, blunted irreparably perhaps, by the fatigue, the last vestiges of vigilance having been drained away from my brain which was now little more than a well of finely dissipated agony inside my head, every strand of muscle, every nerve, drawn tightly into a mass of pressure, pulled together into a net of pain that throbbed behind my temples.

It was curiously difficult to keep my eyes open. The lids seemed leaden, jerking and twitching spasmodically. A little muscle was jumping uncontrollably in my cheek and the back of my throat felt dry and parched.

After a moment, I climbed down from the cockpit, stood on the wing for a moment and glanced round at the others. Most of the planes seemed to be down safely. One was just on the point of touching down at the far end of the runway as I looked up. It was a perfect landing, wheels touching simultaneously.

I smiled faintly to myself in satisfaction, then dropped to the ground. One of the ground crew lifted his shoulders in the ghost of a shrug.

"Looks as though you found what you were looking for, sir."

I nodded. "American convoy heading towards the front," I said briefly. "The cloud base was pretty low, less than five hundred feet, and they never knew what hit them before we were on top of them and away."

"Tanks, sir?" asked one of the other men.

I nodded again. "Mostly tanks, but several trucks, one of them an ammunition truck. It went up in a single explosion that must have disintegrated it completely. There was nothing left of it five minutes later."

"That's quite a good haul, sir, considering the fact that you're not supposed to be doing work like that. Shooting up enemy convoys ought to be the task of the light bombers."

"Unfortunately, there doesn't seem to be any of them to spare right now."

I steadied myself against the fuselage of the plane for a moment, my body jerking spasmodically every few seconds, my mind wandering ahead of my body, trying to think things out, to cut through all of the dead and superfluous thoughts that cluttered my brain and to work out everything clearly.

Every muscle and fibre of my body ached intolerably, my skin soaked with running streams of perspiration, my clothing sticking uncomfortably to my flesh. Each individual cell of my being felt as though a thousand lice were crawling over it and the itch was fast becoming unbearable.

The languid claws of febrile fatigue were settling through my legs and there was fear in my mind somewhere, but I knew not of what I was afraid and the fear was rapidly becoming overlaid by the last stages of complete exhaustion, thrust into the background of a mind that rebelled at having to continue to think, that had been drugged into a semi-stupor by the terrible and soul-destroying tiredness which had been with me for a long time and which nothing, it seemed, could dispel.

How the others continued to stick it, Jensen keeping all of us uppermost in his mind, caring little for his own personal safety, determined that so long as he was around, he would not lose one more pilot or machine than was absolutely necessary.

One of the ground crew personnel cleared his throat noisily and glanced across at me. He wiped the back of his hand across his forehead, then grinned wearily.

"The Commandant asked that you should report to him as soon as you landed, sir," he said stiffly.

"Just me?" I asked, looking surprised.

"No. Every one of the pilots."

"Very well." I was worried, deep down inside by something which I couldn't explain, but I didn't want to show it.

I had a funny feeling in my bones that said we were in for trouble, but it was nothing concrete, merely a hunch. Jensen was walking towards me and I waited for him to come up to me. Deliberately, I thrust away the feeling of apprehension in my mind. This wasn't the way to be thinking, I reflected wearily, even though we were all so dead beat with fatigue and tension that we could scarcely think straight.

"Everybody down?" I asked.

"All except Eberbach. No sign of him, I'm afraid. Come to think of it, I don't remember seeing anything of him after we climbed into the clouds at the conclusion of the attack."

I tried to rack my brains in an attempt to remember, but there was no memory there that I could trust. I remembered Eberbach's plane going in for the second run, but after that there was nothing definite. It was possible, of course, that his plane had been hit and he had been forced to fall behind the rest of us on the way back; but if he had to remain airborne for much longer than another hour, he would be running dangerously short of petrol and might have to make a crash-landing somewhere.

"We'll check with the Commandant and then go over to the Radio Control Unit. They may have picked up a call from him. Anyway, if he is on his way in, he'll have to get in touch with them before he can land, unless his radio had been put out of commission."

"That's possible, of course," I admitted. "But somehow, I think it must be more than that. It's funny that we didn't see him after climbing on course to come back. And if he was hit, you would think that someone must have seen him going down."

"We'll have a word with the others once we're through with the Commandant. Come along, we mustn't keep him waiting. Eberbach may have landed by then."

The interrogation with the Commandant lasted for the best part of thirty-five minutes. He asked us pertinent questions concerning the low-level attack we had carried out, probed deeply into the most minute details, obviously a man who knew what mattered and what didn't where these things were concerned, going to the core of the matter instantly.

By the time he had finished, I felt as though I had undergone an intense session of gruelling by the Gestapo. I was glad to get outside again and breathe the cold, damp air down into my lungs. Jensen lit a cigarette and stood on the concrete apron, his face twisted into a grimace of indecision.

"God, but I hope we don't have to go through anything like that every time we get back from an attack," he said, speaking through a cloud of blue smoke. "He wanted to know everything."

"What about Eberbach," I said softly. "Don't you think we ought to find out something about him. He's over three-quarters of an hour overdue already. He can't last much longer up there if he's still in the air."

"And if he isn't—"

"Then he must have been shot down during the attack itself," I said with conviction. "There was some fire coming up at us, I noticed. Those trucks at the front of the convoy, those which had pulled ahead to the bend in the road. They were pumping shells up at us on the run in. I noticed it both times."

"You reckon he may have been unlucky and been hit by shell-fire?" asked Albrecht.

"It's possible. Can you think of any other explanation?"

He shook his head slowly, pursing his lips. "None at all, I'm afraid. But it scarcely seems credible that he should be dead, if that's what you're suggesting."

"I didn't say he was dead," I muttered defensively. "I merely doubted whether he was still airborne. Unless he lands within a quarter of an hour, he'll find himself with precious little petrol."

"We'll have a word with Radio Control," said Jensen

decisively. "That way, we'll be sure. He may have called up to say that he's been forced down. He may have had to land at some other airfield. There are several things that can have happened to him and it's no use jumping to foregone conclusions."

The Radio Control Section was situated beside the Control Block on the edge of the perimeter track some fifty yards from the hangar. The two operators were seated behind their banks of instruments, earphones clamped down tightly over their ears. Neither of them glanced up as we entered and it was doubtful whether they had heard us.

Eberbach had to be up there somewhere, I thought. Perhaps he had been forced to fall behind because of some simple mechanical failure. A block fuel pipe or a leak. It could have been anything. But I knew, inwardly, that I was merely deluding myself, trying to make my mind avoid the inevitable, refusing to face the facts.

Jensen touched the nearer of the two men on the shoulder. He turned abruptly, blinking up at him, then slowly removed the earphones from his head.

"Any news of one of our aircraft. Went out with us on that tank attack. We got back almost an hour ago, but so far, there's been no sign of him."

The other shook his head. "Nothing come through on this particular channel, sir," he said carefully. "There may have been something on the other though. Carl can tell you about that. He talked the rest of you down when you arrived. If there is one of your planes still up there, he ought to be in contact with him unless his radio is out of order."

"Thanks."

The operator slipped the headphones over his ears again as we moved away, twiddling with the knobs and dials on the bank of instruments in front of him. I dimly heard him say something into the hand microphone as I followed the others to the back of the room where the second operator sat before a transmitting-receiving unit similar to that we had just seen.

Jensen repeated his question to the second man and we stood expectantly.

The operator nodded, slipped the headphones off his head but retained one close to his right ear. He nodded. "Yes, sir, he's still out there somewhere. I've been in contact with him for almost ten minutes, but there seems to be something wrong with his receiver. He keeps sending out calls for information, but he doesn't seem to be answering me. Either he can't pick us up, or he's so scared he doesn't know what he's doing and he's flying without his transmitting button depressed."

"That doesn't seem likely," muttered Jensen slowly, "knowing Eberbach, I doubt whether he would panic like that. After all, he's an experienced and dependable pilot. He wouldn't overlook anything quite as obvious as that."

"Better listen for yourself, sir," suggested the other. "I'll switch it through to the loudspeaker." He flicked over a switch in front of him and sat back in his chair.

"Control to Yellow Four," he said tightly. "Control to Yellow Four. What is your present position. Repeat, what is your present position. Over."

I waited tensely. Only a faint crackling came through the loudspeaker, overlaid on a background hum. For a long moment, there was nothing, then, abruptly shocking in its loudness and clarity, I heard Eberbach's voice:

"Yellow Four to Bitburg Control. Yellow Four to Bitburg Control. Can you hear me? Cannot estimate my position and am not certain about the transmitting equipment. Can you receive me? Can you receive me? Over."

The operator shrugged, flicked the switch of his transmitter and repeated monotonously: "Bitburg Control to Yellow Four. Control to Yellow Four. Receiving you very clearly. Understand transmitter unit not operating satisfactorily. Have been calling you for twenty minutes. Can you hear me now? Over."

"There must be something wrong with his receiver," I said harshly. "He isn't picking you up at all."

"But his transmitter is working perfectly," pointed out Albrecht.

Jensen turned to the operator. "Is it possible for that to happen? I mean, can his transmitter continue functioning satisfactorily while his receiver is faulty?"

The other hesitated, then nodded. "It's possible, I suppose, sir. But very unlikely unless the equipment wasn't checked properly before take-off. I doubt whether any material damage, by shell-fire for example, could have been so selective."

"Then I don't know what to think." Jensen looked perplexed. He stared intently at the transmitter as though expecting to find the answer there, then shrugged his shoulders wearily and turned away. "There was nothing wrong with his receiver during the attack. He obeyed all of the orders given to the letter. Something must have happened afterwards. And now he's out there, probably circling in that cloud, trying to find his way in, wondering why he can't hear from us."

"He can't be so very far away, sir," said the operator after a momentary pause.

Jensen whirled on him sharply. "How can you be so sure of that?" he demanded harshly.

"Nothing definite, sir. But at this job, you get used to judging distances by the strength of the signals. At a guess, I'd say he was within five miles of the airfield at this very minute."

"Five miles," echoed Albrecht. He shook his head in angry despair. "So near and yet so far."

"So long as he keeps coming in this direction, he'll be all right," I said softly. "The cloud is pretty thin here and he ought to be able to pick out the airfield."

"Try to get in touch with him again," muttered Jensen wearily, passing one hand over his brow in a gesture of futility. "It may be that this defect is only temporary. If it is, we might get through to him in time. He can only have petrol for a few more minutes."

"Then he's got to land somewhere," I said, "and the country around here isn't conducive to a safe landing at the best of times; and we've got no idea how badly his plane is shot up. If that's badly hit, a crash landing could be fatal."

"Is the crash tender and ambulance standing by?" snapped Jensen.

The operator nodded his head emphatically. "They'll be ready out there by now, sir," he said tightly. He turned his attention back to the transmitter, began sending out his futile signal into the unresponsive air once more, ears straining to pick up the slightest whisper of radio noise above the murmuring whistle of static.

There was nothing. The ether remained dead; and somewhere within a radius of five or ten miles, in some direction, Eberbach was bringing in his plane blind. I wondered what thoughts were going through his mind at that moment. There was no way of making an accurate estimate of how much petrol he had left in his tanks. If they had been hit during the attack, he would have little enough to spare and an incalculable amount may have drained away, reducing his chances of finding the airfield, and increasing the risk of fire if he was forced to make a crash landing somewhere.

I sucked in a deep breath, walked over towards the wide, glass window which gave a panoramic view of the airfield. From there, it ought to be possible to pick him out if he came within sight of the airfield. But there seemed to be so many imponderables attached to this, that I could feel the bitterness of despair rising in my mouth, threatening to choke me.

"He's still there," called the operator. He looked round and there was a vague expression of surprise on his thin features. "Still can't pick us up though, I'm afraid."

"Never mind. Keep trying," said Jensen sharply. Strain and tension edged his voice, thinning it perceptibly.

I glanced back out of the window, saw the sudden shape that appeared for a moment through a break in the clouds. It was gone before I could make it out properly, but there had been not the slightest doubt in my mind what it was.

"There he is." I was vaguely aware that I was shouting the words at the top of my voice, harshly, excitedly.

Jensen was standing beside me in an instant, peering over my shoulder. "Are you sure?"

"Positive. Can't you hear him?"

We stood quite still, scarcely daring to breathe for a long moment. At first, there was nothing; then gradually, the faint sound of aero engines reached our ears. Jensen relaxed visibly.

"You're sure it was him?"

Before I could answer, he had turned sharply and was facing the radio operator. "Are there any other planes due to land here?" he demanded harshly.

The other shook his head. "Not unless it's another aircraft in distress," he said soberly.

"That's stretching coincidence a little too far, I hope." Jensen turned back to the window. There was a clear patch in the clouds a quarter of a mile to the north of the airfield and we kept our gaze fixed on this. If he came in from any other direction, we would not be able to pick him out through the clouds.

A minute passed, then two. The drone of the aircraft engines was still audible, coming closer at intervals, then fading into the distance.

"He ought to have been able to pick out the airfield through that break in the clouds," I said slowly.

"Then why the devil doesn't he come in to land?" Jensen craned his head forward, peered through the glass, then gave a low mutter of exasperation and walked quickly to the door. After a moment, I followed him.

"Over there!" Albrecht pointed. "There he is!"

Over on the right, beyond the outer markers, appeared the shape of a plane. Here, the clouds were thin and wispy and the fighter was clearly visible.

"He's been hit pretty badly," muttered Jensen. He seemed to be speaking to himself, his lips scarcely moving. His eyes were following the approaching plane, his face expressionless. But for the gradual change of direction of his head and the lowering of his eyelids, he might have been carved from a block of stone. The immobility of his face and the utter stillness of the rest of his body was almost frightening.

There was neither a flicker of emotion, or a look of feeling on his features. What was he thinking of, I wondered, standing there, his whole being strained as if in rigor, almost as if he were willing Eberbach to land the plane safely.

The approach was almost perfect. Slowly and gently, he turned in onto the runway, the wings dipping slightly, then straightening.

"He's going to make it after all," said Albrecht in a

hushed whisper. "He's going to make it."

For a long moment, it looked as though the other was right, as if Eberbach, even under those conditions, *was* going to make it.

But that was not to be. Even as he began to glide down towards the end of the runway, I realised that the under-carriage was still up and locked in position.

He came in at a little over a hundred feet, still holding the plane level, the nose up a little, the drone of the engine sounding louder now, blown to us by the wind. Then, quite suddenly, there was an abrupt change in the note of the straining engine. It rose shrilling for an instant, seemed to scream clamourously at our ears, then cut out altogether.

The nose went down and the machine seemed to falter in mid-air. Steadying myself against the wall of the Radio Building, I forced myself to watch, even though I knew the inevitable outcome. Eberbach was desperately trying to keep the plane's nose up, to cut the speed and level out over the centre of the runway, but it was equally obvious that he would never make it.

Had the fuel lasted for a couple of seconds longer, there might have been a chance. Had he not circled before coming in on his final approach, he would have made it comfortably. As it was, the nose went down suddenly, one wing-tip reached down and touched the grass at the edge of the runway, seemed to catch in the ground as though an invisible hand had grabbed it, pulling it to a standstill while the rest of the plane continued forward under its own terrible momentum.

It slewed round violently, seemed to buck and pitch forward completely out of control. Long afterwards, I was never able to describe what happened next with any degree of accuracy. Memory seemed to cloud it over, to make the sequence of events a hazy blur in my mind. Shocked and stunned, I was vaguely aware of the plane turning over and over along the runway, breaking up as it lurched over the clawing concrete which was swiftly tearing the bottom out of it.

I watched, fascinated. This was the first time I had even seen anything even remotely like this, and I felt appalled.

The entire structure came to rest a hundred yards from the nearer end of the runway, a twisted, unbelievable mass of tangled steel. The first plume of smoke started to rise from this incredible wreck as the fire-tender roared out across the muddy grass.

CHAPTER VIII

In Support

There was nothing we could do. The fire-tender reached the crashed plane seconds ahead of the ambulance and the men were leading out the snaking hoses within moments. Foam sprayed white over the wreck, covering it like a chysalis, bathing it beneath a rippling carpet that almost blotted it out completely.

The danger from fire was still there, I noticed. The plume of smoke still climbed up out of the twisted wreckage, but already, men were clambering forward, walking through the streaming foam, reaching up over the bent wings towards the cockpit. If Eberbach was still alive, which seemed impossible on the surface of things, there was just the chance that they might manage to get him out in one piece.

There was a sudden gush of red tongued flame, rising up swiftly some ten feet behind the cockpit. It seemed incredible that the men could continue to search for the pilot with that raging inferno blazing away only a hair's breadth from them, but continue they did. It seemed to me, watching from the Control Block, as though they never even noticed it, were unaware of the danger; or that if they were, they left it to the remainder of the firemen to deal with and concentrated on the task in hand.

A moment later, they had reached the cockpit, had hacked at it with blue-edged steel, smashing the plastic under a series of hammer blows. There was no time now for finesse. Everything had to be done as quickly as possible if the pilot was to stand chance at all of survival.

"He's out," breathed Albrecht in a hoarse whisper.

"They've got him out."

"But what kind of shape is he in?" murmured Jensen soberly. "After that landing. I think his chances are almost nil."

"It may have looked worse than it actually was," I muttered thinly. Deep down inside, I knew that this wasn't so; that it was the tired brain, not wanting to believe, trying to tip the scales against reason and logic.

"We'll soon find out," Albrecht pointed. "They've got him down into the ambulance."

A few seconds later, the ambulance moved away from the still smouldering wreck and headed swiftly towards the main buildings. In my mind's eye, I could visualise Eberbach's pain-wracked body swaying agonisingly against the supports as they bumped their way across the airfield.

"It'll be half an hour before we know anything definite," said Jensen sharply. His voice sounded strangely high-pitched for so big a man. "Better get some rest while we have the chance."

Slowly, we made our way back to the billets. It was beginning to drizzle again and the clouds were lowering swiftly. Very soon, it would be completely overcast. On the runway, the wreckage was still smouldering, but all danger of fire seemed to have been averted.

*   *   *   *

It was still raining heavily as I made my way through the brown mud towards the Sick Bay. There had been no word of Eberbach's condition since we had seen him being taken away in the ambulance and almost three-quarters of an hour had passed. It was quite dark now, a miserable, wet darkness, unlit by a solitary star.

Not a flicker of light showed through the heavy draperies over the windows of the field hospital and I was totally unprepared for the blaze of actinic radiation which hit me as I opened the swing doors at the end of the short corridor and pushed my way through. Gradually, my vision steadied itself and the rest of the small room swam into view as I stood there, blinking rapidly. One of the orderlies sat behind a small wooden desk and glanced up curiously as I entered, pen in hand.

"Did you wish to see someone, sir?" he said differentially.

"I'd like to know how the pilot is they brought in almost an hour ago," I said, licking my lips. There was the sharp, sickly-sweet smell of antiseptic and ether hanging in the room and through the glass-panelled door I could see directly into the ward. Most of the beds, I noticed, with a profound shock, were already occupied. Then I recalled the bitter fighting which was going on at the front less than thirty miles from there and knew that these were, in all probability, some of the casualties, brought here for the want of any other place to go.

"Lieutenant Eberbach. Is that it, sir?"

"Eh, what was that?" I turned to look at him, scarcely hearing what he said.

"The pilot who was brought here a little while ago after his plane crashed on the airfield."

"Yes, yes. That's right. May I see him?"

The other got slowly to his feet, walked forward. "I'm afraid I'll have to speak with Doctor Faber first, sir," he said briskly. "He's in charge of the ward. The pilot was very badly injured and it may be possible that the doctor does not wish him to receive any visitors at the moment. If you'll just wait here for a moment, I'll see him."

"Thank you."

The other went through the swing doors and walked along the ward until he reached a small door at the far end. Walking through this, he closed it behind him. The air inside the room was cold and still—motionless, and I was vaguely aware of my own heart thumping madly against my ribs. There was a faint, but continuous pounding in my ears which I forced myself to ignore.

The white-painted ceiling, with the long, fluorescent lights set close to it, throwing no shadows, seemed oddly out of place here. In a large hospital in Berlin or in one of the other cities, I could have imagined it, but not here.

The orderly came back a moment later and there was a short stocky man behind him, his balding head glistening a little in the harsh light. He had a pair of rimless spectacles balanced precariously on his nose and he glanced over them at me with a suspicious glint in his steel-blue eyes.

"I understand that you wish to inquire about Lieutenant Eberbach," he said nasally.

I nodded. "That's right. He belonged to my squadron. He crashed this afternoon. How is he?"

"As well as could be expected, I suppose, considering what he's been through. I believe the plane was literally smashed to pieces."

"It was pretty badly wrecked, I'll admit," I said softly. The orderly had seated himself behind the desk and was regarding us curiously, his hands placed on the table in front of him, lips touching.

"So it would seem." The other drew himself up to his full height and pursed his lips. "I think I ought to tell you now, that your friend is very seriously injured."

"But he's going to live? He'll pull through?"

"That is still a matter of conjecture, I'm afraid. We've done the best we can for him, naturally. The rest is out of our hands entirely. He had a strong constitution at one time, I can tell that, but the strain he's obviously been through during the past few months has lowered his strength and resistance almost to vanishing point. That's one of the things we have to contend with, I'm afraid, especially as far as pilots are concerned. Lack of sleep, lack of proper food, can soon reduce a man to a pitiful state. If anything like this happens to a man in that terrible physical and mental condition, there is usually very little we can do for them. All of our drugs and surgery can be of little avail, if he himself has nothing left with which to fight."

"I think I understand, doctor."

He smiled faintly, but the smile never went further than his thin, almost bloodless, lips. "Do you? I wonder. If you'd seen as many poor creatures as I have, you'd cease to be surprised at anything. These creatures that we get in here every day, were once men. Now they are empty shells. They've lost the will to go on living, together with the ability to fight. Without both of these things, our task is virtually hopeless."

"And Eberbach?" I prompted, bringing him back to his original subject. "How does he stand?"

"Not too well. He rallied after the first transfusion, but there are second and third degree burns on almost every part of his body. It's almost impossible to describe his condition to anyone who has not seen it for himself. In addition, he had three bullet wounds, two in the right shoulder, fortunately missing both lung and heart by less than an inch, and the third in his left thigh. Under normal circumstances, none of these would present any problem to us.

"But in his terribly weakened condition, and taking into account the blood he has undeniably lost, I don't hold out much hope for him. He may live through the night and into tomorrow. But beyond that, it is impossible to tell."

Quite suddenly, I was conscious of a dreadful, nameless chill which struck at my body. I knew by some sense deep within me, that the doctor was telling the plain, unvarnished truth, that there was little hope for Eberbach. But my mind refused to take it all in at once, as if by rejecting the inevitable, it could postpone it, or even remove it altogether.

"Would it be possible to see him?" I asked, trying to keep my voice steady.

The other hesitated and rubbed his fingers over his chin reflectively. Then he nodded. "I think that might be arranged," he said thinly. "After all, if my ideas are correct and he does not have very long to live, your seeing him cannot have any effect on him, good or otherwise."

"Thank you, doctor."

The other turned on his heel, pushed open the swing doors with the flat of his hand and held them open for me to follow him. The smell of ether struck me more forcibly as I stepped through into the ward and followed close on the other's heels.

Every bed seemed to be occupied. Most of the men, I noticed immediately, were seriously wounded. Here and there, screens had been placed round a bed and behind one of them, a man was moaning piteously, occasionally screaming out aloud with a shrieking noise that was heart-stopping.

The doctor walked right through the ward and through the door at the far side. Holding it open for me, he said by way of explanation:

"We're keeping Lieutenant Eberbach through here in one of the smaller wards. Most of the men through there in the main ward were brought in late this afternoon from the front line. Every hospital seemed to be filled to over-flowing with the wounded. Very soon, we ourselves, will have to turn them away. This is a terrible war we're fighting. If it doesn't end soon, there'll be no young men left alive in the country and Germany will be completely reduced to a land of cripples and old men."

I glanced about me hurriedly, surprised at the vehemence and depth of feeling in the other's voice. Shocked almost, I listened as he went on:

"If only the people could realise where the so-called leaders of this country are leading them, there would be another revolution inside Germany. By continuing to fight, they're asking for total annihilation. We can't continue to struggle against an enemy so much stronger to us in men and materials. What is the Feuhrer depending on? A miracle? If so, I'm afraid he's going to be disappointed."

"Isn't it dangerous to talk like that?" I said harshly. "Men have been shot for sedition, you know."

He nodded his head wearily. "I know. I know, you don't need to remind me of that. I've seen too much of it during my lifetime to be afraid of it any longer. I'm an old man, you know, and my life, as such, is nearly ended. If they choose to shoot me simply because I recognise the truth and am not afraid to speak it out to the world, then let them do so."

"And your family? What about them?"

"My family." There was a touch of some emotion I couldn't quite define in his steady voice. It was not quite anger, or weariness, or plain despair, but rather a blend of them all. "My wife and son were in Berlin at the beginning of the year when the R.A.F. bombed the city. A cluster of high explosive bombs fell on the house and destroyed it completely. At least, they never had time to suffer. A split second and it was all over for them. But not for me. I'm left behind. It is I who have to suffer now."

"And why don't you blame the R.A.F.?"

"You can't blame their death on an inanimate thing

like a bomb, even less on the unknown man who pressed the bomb release and dropped it from somewhere high above the clouds, seeing only a mass of blue on his radar screen. No—the only people who can really be blamed are those who led Germany into this disastrous war."

He paused, shook his head slowly and sadly, then pushed open a further door at the end of the short passage and ushered me through. Here, the lighting was far more subdued, a welcome change after the harsh, eye-searing brilliance of the main ward outside. I glanced about me.

There were seven beds in the small room, four of them occupied, the remainder standing empty, the sheets folded neatly over them. Two of the men were sitting propped up on high pillows, the third, lying flat on his back, his face swathed in bandages, was obviously Eberbach.

Slowly, I walked towards the bed and stood at the foot of it in shocked silence. My brain felt empty and strange, stunned almost. Drawing in a single breath, I looked around at the doctor standing at my side, vaguely aware of the look of horror which must have been imprinted upon my cold face.

"We've given him an injection of morphia," explained the other. "It will keep him under for several hours yet. He feels no pain. and I doubt whether he has recovered consciousness since he was brought in here."

"And you really believe there's no hope for him, doctor?"

The other spread his hands in a futile gesture. "Who can say? If it were left up to me, I would say, definitely, no. He cannot live until morning. It is a miracle that he is still alive. By rights, he ought to have died when that plane crashed. Somehow, he remains alive and it is our duty to keep him alive as long as we can."

"I realise that, doctor." I looked away from the other, down at the bandaged figure on the bed. His body seemed to be grotesquely swollen, but that I put down to my imagination and the effect of the bandages.

"I wonder if he knows?" I said quietly, speaking my thoughts out aloud.

"That he's going to die?" queried the doctor, turning his head and looking at me queerly.

"Well . . . yes."

He pursed his lips. "I think he must have had a good idea when he tried to bring that plane in," he muttered finally. "He must have known that he didn't stand much of a chance."

"Yes, you're right, I suppose." I nodded my head mechanically, moved forward a little to take a better look at the other. The bandages covered most of the top half of his body, were wrapped completely around his shoulders, covered most of his face, although his eyes, nose and mouth were still visible.

"God—what a mess," I said after a brief pause. There was a feeling of intense despair in me at that moment. Oh Hell, was it all worth it? Did it mean anything that men like this should go out and die for nothing? I felt helpless, unable to do anything to help in the slightest degree.

Even though I didn't want to keep on putting my innermost thoughts into words, I suddenly blurted out:

"He never stood a chance from the very beginning, did he, doctor?" It sounded like a sacrilege, but it had to be said.

The other's tired, twisted grin was deceptive. His face was a grey mask of professional non-committal. "I don't know," he said finally, simply, "there are some things we couldn't possibly take into account. Several complications are likely to set in, in a case such as this, you know. Secondary infections which although quite innocuous under normal conditions, could be rapidly fatal in this case."

"How long before the drug wears off?"

"Three, four hours, maybe."

"And then you'll have to give him some more."

"Yes. Otherwise, he would probably die of the shock and the agony. I'm quite certain that the pain could have brought on fatal shock if he hadn't been injected the moment he arrived here."

He adjusted one of the bandages on the injured man's head, his touch gentle and amazingly tender, almost caressing. The expression on his tight face was one I had never seen before.

"Maybe it would have been better if we had left him there in that plane to be burned to a crisp," I said, feeling my throat tight and constricted. "I know it's a hard and callous thing to say, but you admitted yourself that there was nothing you, or anybody else, could do for him. What do we gain by dragging him out and allowing him to linger on like this? A few precious hours? But precious to whom? Certainly not to him."

"Steady, steady." The other laid his hand on my arm and turned me round gently, away from the bed. "That isn't the way to look at things. I know it's very hard at first, but when you've seen as many men die as I have, you realise that there has to be a purpose behind it. I bear no grudge against the bomb aimer who killed my wife and children. There is too much hatred in this world, too many people intent on killing and destroying. One day, sanity must prevail and then will come the time for re-building, for re-populating the world, and I pray to God every night, every time I see one of these poor devils being brought in here, that the time for peace is not far off, even if Germany has to lose this terrible war, and that people will never allow themselves to degenerate to the level of animals again. Self-abasement, that's all it is."

I nodded numbly. War was a terrible thing, but I had never heard the argument put so vehemently or so convincingly as that. The other sounded tired as he spoke and his face was very stiff and cold as he gripped my arm more tightly and led me, unresisting, towards the door.

I swallowed hard and nodded briefly. "I'm all right now, doctor. Sorry I allowed myself to let go like that. I'm all right, really I am."

"We'll let you know when it happens," he said gently. As we reached the door, he threw a swift glance over his shoulder towards the bed where Eberbach lay wrapped like a mummy in the bandages.

"Somehow, I don't think it will be very long now."

CHAPTER IX

The Battle Continues . . .

Lieutenant Eberbach, pilot of the Luftwaffe, died an hour after dawn, the following morning. Both Jensen and I were present when he died. The cause of death was officially given as extensive third-degree burns coupled with post-operative shock arising from multiple bullet wounds.

The truth, to my mind, was far different. It was simply that Eberbach had no will left to continue the fight for life. That all of the mental and physical strength had been drained out of him by the continual exposure to tension and fear, that there had been no chance of life for him ever since he had joined the squadron some eighteen months earlier and that his death, and the cause of it, if cause were needed, could be traced back to a continual succession of tiny, seemingly insignificant events which, taken together, had sapped his resistance to nothing.

For a moment before he died, it seemed that he regained consciousness. His eyes, half-hidden beneath the mask of bandages and acriflavine cream, opened and looked directly at us, clearly and without any trace of pain. His lips twitched into a caricature of a smile and for an instant, he tried to raise himself onto his elbows. Then his eyes rolled in his head, his shoulders fell back onto the pillow; and he died.

At three o'clock in the afternoon, as he was being buried in the large cemetery in Bitburg, we were in the air, heading westwards towards the rolling, tree-covered country of the Ardennes in support of the Army as it moved westwards, thrusting savagely at the enemy who still seemed to be demoralised, uncertain of the position.

Here and there, small groups of American soldiers were holding out, especially in the Bordeaux area, and our task was to make things as untenable as possible for them. This time, bombs had been fitted in special racks under the wings, the cannon had been loaded to maximum capacity, and there was petrol to spare in the tanks.

For the moment, the battle was going in our favour and it was essential that everything in our power should be done to preserve the initiative. Nothing had been spared to make this mission a success.

We took off at a few minutes before three, climbing steeply into the clouds that still hung low over the entire area. I turned my head slightly from side to side as we came out of the cloud, into the sunlight, keeping my eyes moving, never letting them stare at the same point for any length of time. Up here, high above the clouds, it was still light and there was always the chance that, after the attack of the previous day, the enemy had learned their lesson and would fly off their fighters in spite of the weather, in an attempt to prevent the same thing from happening again. If that happened, it could be fatal to fix one's gaze on any one spot.

Clouds hung like bits of foamy sediment all around us, washed up by some invisible, swelling tide onto unseen beaches in the air. Mostly they were below us, almost five hundred feet away, blanketing out the ground completely except at scattered points where they broke up into pieces, scattered and shredded by the turbulence of the wind in the upper atmosphere, allowing us a brief glimpse of browns and greens.

I stared out over the clouds and saw the dark shapes of the other planes flying alongside, standing out starkly against the clearness of the sky.

Something fresh and exhilarating slid down into my body and tensed the muscles of my stomach. The great, powerful engine continued to roar, the shudder and vibration passing into the metal of the plane and then up into my body, setting up a queer, high-pitched singing in my brain.

It was to be the usual routine. One which was completely familiar by now.

Locate the enemy and destroy them utterly. Those were our orders. By the time we were crossing the fighting line and could just make out the flashes of the guns and the faint streaming arrows of ground-to-ground tracer sparkling on the fields below, the excitement had begun to mount. Muscles tensed a little in spite of everything I could do to force myself to relax. My brain began to tick over rapidly, the faint drowsiness of fatigue fading away rapidly. It was difficult to believe that in each of these sleek, dark shapes beside me, men were sitting tensed like myself, squatting behind the controls, their fingers ready on the firing buttons in case the enemy fighters were in the area, waiting to pounce upon us before we were aware of their presence.

Men with their own individual hopes and fears, filled with prayers and oaths whenever anything went wrong, terror and fear dying and being born anew in them with every operational flight they made; all of them knowing that sooner or later, no matter how lucky they had been in the past, the long arm of fate would catch up with them, bringing their lives and careers to an abrupt and unexpected end.

"Looks as though somebody down there has got sharp eyes, or ears," said Jensen's voice close against my ear.

I glanced down. Flak soared up to reach us, breaking through the tenuous veil of the clouds, bursting dangerously close. From far away, it looked oddly unreal and unsubstantial, strangely red and beautiful, moving up towards us so slowly that it seemed impossible it could ever reach us. But this was an illusion. The nearer it came, the more it seemed to accelerate, whipping past us in streaks of red and orange. The plane lurched and shuddered as several shells exploded close at hand on the same level as myself.

"We'd better take evasive action before they get our range and direction a little more accurately," muttered Jensen again. His voice sounded oddly irritable over the intercom. I tried to analyse the emotions present in it, but was unable to do so. I certainly could not detect any quavering panic in it, but that was nothing to go by.

With an effort, I shook off the feeling of impending disaster. A moment later, I heard Albrecht's calm and unhurried voice saying:

"I propose we get out of this area while we're all still intact. They seem to have only just begun to wake up to things down there. I don't fancy being shot at when they really get going."

Over on the starboard bow, where the cloud was beginning to thicken a little, there was a widespread sprinkling of red and white and orange fire like a sheet of summer lightning, with a cloud of glowing balls, shot through with red, soaring upwards, swooping up in an alarming manner and bursting into expanding spheres of coruscating light all around us.

"Do you think they'll have any fighters up looking for us?" I asked casually.

"Frankly, I doubt it," muttered Jensen. "Not with all this flak flying around. They wouldn't be inclined to shoot down their own planes by mistake."

Following Jensen, we banked steeply to starboard, slid away out of danger, propellers beating at the air, engines roaring incessantly.

My mind, my fingers, seemed to be numb, without feeling of any kind, touching the controls, but not a part of them. The interior of my body seemed far more sensitive than my flesh, but it was sensitive in the way of the flesh. There was little vision among the clouds, but I seemed to need none. My entire world was composed of filmy wisps of grey, interspersed with spitting lines of flak which criss-crossed over my vision in a manner that was both confusing and frightening.

It seemed incredible that I had not been hit. Sharp, stinging odours were in the back of my throat. My mouth seemed to be nothing more than a dry hole through which these vapours passed in and out on their way to and from my lungs.

"They seemed to be following us," shouted Albrecht. I tried to make out which plane was his, but it was impossible to see more than twenty yards in any direction and the others were just vague shapes, visible for a few moments as the clouds parted, then vanishing again.

Occasionally, down below, I could just make out the pinpoints of light which marked the position of the enemy guns still mercilessly pumping shells into the air, following us as we banked and climbed to avoid their fire. The accuracy of their gunnery was quite fantastic.

With an effort, I tore my gaze away from the rippling sheet of winking flame and concentrated on flying the aircraft out of that terrible crossfire. I altered course slowly, gingerly, feeling the clouds and the danger close in about me outside. There was that peculiar tensed sensation of knowing that death lay very close, waiting to reach in whenever I least expected it. There was also a feeling of utter helplessness which was even worse.

I was acutely aware of the hardness of the seat against my back and shoulder blades and the firm touch of the control column between my fingers as I held it tightly in my hands. I was physically conscious to a very marked degree of every slight noise and small movement of the plane. Feeling seemed to be magnified beyond all comprehension.

Carefully, I pulled out of the climb, levelled off. Once again, the cloud was all below me and I could see the others clearly. Quite suddenly, I realised the weight and roughness of the clothing on my limbs, became conscious of the soft rub of it against my skin. There was the feeling that any sudden noise, any untoward noise would be an intolerable, unbearable agony.

And mixed with this strange dread, overriding it all, there remained the terrible fear of dying. Of being shot to pieces by the exploding shells, mangled and ripped by the concussive force of the explosion, simply for the sake of dropping a few more hundred pounds of high explosive onto the convoys down there, moving up swiftly towards the front, hoping to stem the tide of our advance before things really got out of hand.

What good would it all do? I wondered. And above all, was it worth the risk? I suddenly remembered Eberbach, lying there on that hospital bed, his body swathed in bandages, his limbs wracked by a terrible pain, mitigated only to some small extent by the morphia and loss of consciousness.

It just did not seem to be worth the risk. For all of our lives to be suddenly and irrevocably cancelled out by some American gunner who simply happened to tighten his finger on the firing mechanism of an anti-aircraft gun at precisely the right instant, with the barrel of the gun pointing in exactly the right direction; and possibly not knowing that the particular shell he had just fired had hit the target.

Even though I tried desperately to remind myself that every single bomb dropped on the enemy convoys, every shell that destroyed one of their trucks, would help to swing events in Germany's favour, although I attempted to replace the suddenly personal by the strictly impersonal, trying to bring everything into its proper perspective, some of the surging bitterness still remained in my mouth.

Jensen's voice broke in on my thoughts. "We seem to have left them behind for the time being. Either that, or they've lost us in the clouds. We must remember to look out for them on the way back. It's highly likely that they'll be waiting for us."

"The cloud is thinning quite appreciably down there, too," said Albrecht.

I glanced down over the rim of the cockpit. The sunlight, striking in a wide net through breaks in the cloud, lit up the ground with an overall hazy green, picking out the lacework of roads clearly so that everything stood out in stark relief. Woods stood in shadow, contours emerging from the general background pattern of fields and hedges.

"Looks peaceful down there," I observed. "No sign of movement anywhere. Could be they've learned their lesson after yesterday and are moving them up under cover of darkness."

"They can't afford to do that," reminded Jensen. "There's a full-scale attack going on down there and the Americans are on the receiving end for a change. They won't like that; and knowing them, they'll push through everything they possibly can to reinforce their troops at the front. Even if they have to escort their convoys with a battery of anti-aircraft guns."

"Well, they don't seem too active at the moment," I went on defensively.

"Let's go down and take a good look. I'm getting used to surprises by now. Maybe they're not using the main roads, but are trying to get them through along the lanes. There would be more cover there."

Gently, I put the nose of the plane down, heard the thin scream of the wind around the fuselage, saw the ground come up to meet me. Everything began to expand outwards with a terrifying speed from the central point directly below me. Details emerged from the general haze of colour, angles and contours resolved themselves, roads stood out more clearly, shadows touched and outlined the hedges that parcelled off the fields into neat little squares.

The rugged outlines of some high hills stretched away to the north and I kept a wary eye on them. But immediately below, the ground was flat and reasonably smooth, with few obstacles.

We followed the enemy's main supply route through that sector for a couple of miles, eyes peeled, watching closely for anything that moved. For most of that distance, the road was empty, deserted, except for an occasional truck speeding in the opposite direction, away from the front; and once, we spotted an ambulance with its red cross a vivid splash of colour, painted on the roof of the vehicle.

We left these vehicles strictly alone. The trucks we wanted would be moving towards the fighting line. Those going away would undoubtedly be empty and we had little enough ammunition to waste it on such targets.

Ten minutes later, we spotted them, a long string of vehicles moving slowly eastwards, keeping well in to the side of the narrow, twisting road. Directly ahead of them, the highway curved back on itself like a snake's back, riding high over the edge of a steep valley. On the opposite side of the road, there was a rocky escarpment, thickly wooded at the top which would make things difficult for us.

"There they are," said Jensen exultantly. His voice sounded oddly loud and metallic over the intercom. "There must be close on fifty trucks in that convoy."

"Maybe so," I said soberly, "but take a good look at that hill on the far side of the road. If they take it into their heads to open fire on us as we go in, we won't be able to take much evasive action. One wrong move, and we could pile up on those rocks before we knew about it."

"That's a risk we'll have to take. This chance is too good to miss. We'll run in along the road itself. That ought to give us the maximum clear run, time to drop these bombs and get out of the way."

I remained silent. It wasn't going to be quite as simple

as that. The presence of the high ground meant that we would have to attack the convoy at an angle, drop our bombs and turn away steeply, climbing at the same time.

I shuddered at the thought of what would happen if one of us made the slightest slip on that dangerous run in. The hilly ground would be waiting to mash us to pieces if we overshot the convoy by so much as ten yards; but there was the point that this was the one spot along the whole three miles of highway where the enemy would not expect us to attack.

Glancing down at them again, I saw that the leading trucks were accelerating; trying to reach the sharply-angled bend where they considered they would be safe. I wondered whether any of those vehicles down there possessed a radio transmitter. If they did, it was also highly likely that, even at that moment, while we were waiting for them to get into position, someone was sitting in front of the instrument, sending an urgent message to their nearest airfield, asking for help. For all we knew, time could be running out very quickly indeed.

I corrected the course of the plane slightly as Jensen's aircraft suddenly flipped over on one wing-tip and dived steeply. Without a moment's hesitation, I corrected again, then went down after him. The hills loomed up dangerously close on the starboard bow, rising up above me as I went down to little more than a hundred feet. The leading trucks of the convoy had swung around the S-bend and were pulling in to the side.

Even as I thumbed the bomb release switch, I saw them skid to a halt, some almost in the ditch. Doors swung open as the drivers dropped out and ran for the comparative safety of the hedges. Men crawled over the tailboards, dropped onto the road and began running in all directions.

I saw Jensen pulling swiftly out of his dive, banking steeply away from the rising cliffs. The second group of trucks came into my sights and I squeezed the release button instinctively, felt the sudden lurch, the odd lightness as the bomb fell away, then the bare side of the hill scraped by me less than ten yards away as I pulled heavily on the stick.

Ten seconds later, I climbed steeply, swinging away. The plane responded instantly, smoothly. Instinctively, I straightened the plane out onto an even keel, turned slowly and glanced round at the convoy. The trucks had scattered all over the roadway by now and several were on fire. The bombers had done their work well. Judging by the absence of reaction on the part of the enemy, it was clear that we had taken them completely by surprise with the manoeuvre, had completely fooled them as to our intentions.

Seven seconds—seven seconds was time and to spare for a bombing run over a convoy such as that below, attacking them in a shallow dive. There would be barely time for realisation, for the knowledge to penetrate their brains and we would have been upon them before they knew what was happening.

The last of the planes banked steeply away from the rocks and climbed up to join the rest of us. So far, everything had gone off according to plan. But by now, the enemy were fully awake as to our intentions and on the next run-in, when we would rake them with cannon fire, they would be ready for us.

Swinging to the south of the road, I turned the plane onto an interception course, following Jensen again. My arms were aching curiously and there was a dull, nagging pain in my leg that was making itself felt now that I had time in which to notice it. Repeatedly, I tried to relax, telling myself that luck had been with us so far, far more than we had ever deserved, and that there was no real reason why it should not continue. I had seen no sign of heavy artillery attached to this particular convoy on the initial run and it was quite possible that our fears were groundless. The hills presented a problem, but we had escaped them so far and careful navigation should keep us clear of them.

There was a queer taste in my mouth as I put the plane into a shallow dive. The trucks were laid out all over the road, some pulled up in the ditches where their drivers had panicked and had run them off the road at our approach. Others seemed to have been hit as they were moving forward and were piled in heaps of tangled wreckage in the middle of the road, effectively blocking it for those vehicles behind them who were now prevented from reaching the sanctuary of the double bend.

I screwed up my eyes in automatic reflex as I lined up the plane on the convoy, searching the scattered trucks for any sign of return fire. For a long moment, there seemed to be nothing. Then, almost before I was aware of it, I could just see the tiny flashes originating from near the middle of the line of vehicles.

Bringing the nose down sharply, keeping one eye on the hill looming up on my right, I fired a short, exploratory burst, saw the tracer flickering in a line of red darts over the road a little to the right of the trucks. Correcting slightly, I fired a prolonged burst and held the guns on the target for a full four or five seconds while the shells ripped the line of trucks apart.

Men were still running panic-stricken in all directions, but I ignored them completely. It was not the men I was after this time, but the vehicles themselves. Savagely, exultantly, I sprayed them with tracer, saw an expanding ball of flame burst from one of them as I roared low over it. The savage detonation wave hit at the underside of the plane as the truck exploded and I fought desperately for control. Madly, I wrestled with the control column as the plane side-slipped violently, moving towards the rocks less than twenty feet away from the starboard wing-tip.

For a long moment, I had the impression that the air-craft was failing to respond. Seconds dragged themselves by with an incredible slowness, stretching themselves out like individual nightmares of slow motion. Then, slowly but surely, the plane responded to the controls, moved away from the rocks that skimmed by an inch at a time.

How far away were those jagged rocks? A little voice, screaming low down in my mind, urged me to climb steeply, but caution prevailed. It was more than likely that there was an overhang somewhere along the side of the road and any attempt to climb could result only in disaster. With an effort, I controlled the urge, concentrated on keeping to the same height until I had gained sufficient clearance to risk bringing up the nose slightly.

The terror had built up swiftly, eating at my nerves and

bringing in its train a foolish, unreasoning panic which threatened to dominate me. Desperately, I thought: Nobody could even know what it was to sit here like this in a plane moving at close on two hundred and fifty miles an hour, knowing that death lay only a few feet away and that only luck and a little skill and God's good grace could bring me through the terrible moments which lay ahead.

I had never known anything like this before. Even in the throes of terror and panic, I was vaguely aware that I would know nothing about it if I did crash into that hillside. There would be a fraction of a second of light and sound that would have no meaning and then there would be nothing. There would be no suffering, no pain, as Eberbach had suffered.

After what seemed an eternity, I came out into the open, still little more than a hundred feet above the ground, skimming beneath me at an incredible speed. Pulling back on the stick, I climbed swiftly, circling into the clouds. Levelling out at a couple of thousand feet, I leaned back in my seat, aware of the thunderous pounding of the blood in my ears, breathing a little easier.

"What happened to you?" Jensen's voice was shouting urgently in my ear.

I flicked on the transmitting switch of the microphone and said breathlessly. "The blast from that exploding truck must have caught the plane as I passed over it. Threw it out of control for a few seconds. I thought I'd never be able to pull away from that hill."

"I thought you'd been hit. They were firing at us as we went in on that run."

"I know. I saw something coming up towards me, but there wasn't time to see how effective it was."

"Quite effective, I'm afraid." The other's voice was suddenly grim. "As someone's already found out."

I glanced round swiftly. There had been something in the other's tone which brought a sense of impending disaster into my mind. At first, I could see nothing wrong. It was only when I turned my head and glanced behind me that I saw the splash of flame and smoke spread across the darkening sky.

"Who is it?" I asked harshly. Almost immediately, I thought: Oh God, what a stupid, inane thing to say.

"No idea yet." Jensen's voice was soft, almost inaudible, as if he were afraid that the enemy might be listening in on our conversation.

A moment later, we knew. Albrecht failed to answer when Jensen called each one of us in turn. Somewhere in the distance, almost two miles beyond the convoy which had been almost completely destroyed, there was a brilliant, vivid flash on the ground. It spread out swiftly into a big ball of flame that had no features, made no noise, but that was oddly, terrifying significant.

There was a long silence as we began climbing up to five thousand feet, then turned on course.

There wasn't anything to say and it was painfully obvious that nobody wanted to be the first to put our thoughts into words.

The journey back was uneventful. We passed over the area where we had previously run into the heavy flak, but it was growing dark on the ground by this time and apart from a few desultory shots, nothing was fired at us. Thirty minuter later, we landed at the airfield, answered the questions put to us during the brief interrogation, then went back to the billets and lay silently on our bunks, scarcely looking at each other.

CHAPTER X

Retaliation

The daylight missions carried out during the remainder of that week were equally successful as far as destruction of enemy convoys was concerned. Always we succeeded in finding a convoy working its way along the tortuous, twisting roads to the front, always we managed to destroy the greater part of it without loss to ourselves, and even the battle on the ground seemed to be going in our favour.

It was true that we had not taken all of the primary objectives which had been laid down by the Army Commanders, but one thing did resolve itself from the maze of reports that came in every day. The enemy had been hit, and hit hard. Even now, seven days after the attack had been launched, they were still not certain of the position. In several places, the German army had thrust deeply through their defences, had surrounded Bastogne and had split the American front in two.

St. Vith was being assailed from two sides and it was possible that Manteuffel's armour would have a clear run through the enemy lines to Dinant and Namur, where they would soon be on the Meuse.

The Commandant seemed to have regained some of his early good humour and was in high spirits.

"Maybe we really are doing the right thing now, bombing their convoys and preventing supplies and troops getting up to the front," he admitted. He placed a cigarette in the long holder and lit it carefully, leaning back in his chair and crossing his legs. As always, his uniform was immaculately pressed and laundered.

"I wasn't sure of the wisdom of this kind of attack in the beginning," he went on lightly, "but it seems to have the enemy worried. We've suffered losses, I'll admit, but somehow I don't believe that they can continue losing men and materials at this rate for much longer. Already, we have advanced the best part of thirty miles into their defences and driven them back into Belgium."

He blew out a ring of smoke, nodded slowly as though secretly amused at something, then went on softly. "By Christmas Day gentlemen, we shall be over to the Meuse and Antwerp will be in our hands. Without the use of the port, the enemy will be helpless. We shall drive them from Europe, back into Britain. And possibly, we may not stop there. This time, they will have to be taught a lesson."

His eyes seemed unnaturally bright. "In addition, I think this has heightened the morale of all of the men on the airfield. Before this attack, I gained the impression that there was an air of despondency here. Now, all that is changed, drastically. We've had our losses, too, but that is inevitable. Now that the technique has been perfected, all of our planes have returned from these missions."

He broke off suddenly and gazed pensively out through

the window. I watched him narrowly. Somehow, I had the feeling that there was a note of uncertainty under that of supreme confidence which he wanted to impart to us. Almost as if he did not quite believe what he said himself.

He sat in silence for a few moments, elbows on the table, his right hand running through his thinning hair—a favourite mannerism of his. Then he glanced up abruptly.

"What do you think of the situation, Jensen?" he asked briefly.

For a moment, the other seemed to have been caught on the wrong foot by the suddenness of the question, then he straightened a little in his chair, uncrossed his legs and said tightly: "To be quite frank, sir, I'm not as confident about the outcome of these missions as you are."

"Oh?" The Commandant lifted his eyebrows in an interrogatory look of mild surprise. "In what way? Aren't you satisfied with the way things are going?"

Jensen frowned heavily. "It isn't that, sir. I'm just not sure that we have perfected the technique."

"But you've got to admit that for the past five or six days we've lost no planes."

"That's true, sir. But I think that can be ascribed more to luck than to good judgement."

"You're implying that we could go about this thing in a better way?"

"Yes, sir." Jensen licked his lips. "I'm a fighter pilot, sir, as are the rest of us." He smiled faintly. "Maybe we're not the best fighter pilots in the Luftwaffe and perhaps we haven't had the opportunity of keeping abreast with the latest developments in this field, but it does seem to me that we would be better employed in attacking enemy planes and escorting our heavy bombers, than in making these routine, but somehow ineffectual attacks. So we shoot up an enemy convoy every day. But where does it get us. That's a mere drop in the ocean as far as they are concerned. It isn't always easy to locate them, and when we do, it's impossible to tell how effective our attack has been. We see a row of trucks strewn out over the road, some of them on fire, and a few blown to pieces. But how badly are the majority of them damaged and how much of the equipment in them can be readily salvaged by the enemy, the same day?"

The other tapped the ash from the tip of his cigarette with a deliberate motion of his hand, his face hard and emotionless. Then he said, deceptively casually: "I'm afraid I don't quite see what you're getting at."

"Simply this, sir. The proper planes for these attacks are the heavy bombers. We could escort them in and keep a watch for any American fighters in the area while they destroyed the convoy totally. There would be nothing left of it once they had completed a bombing run. The amount of high explosive we can carry is negligible. A single bomber could carry a greater bomb load than the whole of this squadron."

The Commandant grunted, whether in anger or derision, it was impossible to say, and cleared his throat to interrupt, but Jensen went on swiftly:

"Very soon, the enemy are going to get wise to us. In fact, I'm surprised they haven't done so already. There will be fighters waiting for us soon, and it will be impossible for us to take care of them and attack the convoy as well."

"A very interesting hypothesis," said the other after a brief pause. "Very interesting indeed. And most instructive. But there is one point you seem to have overlooked. We do not have the heavy bombers with which to put your plan into operation. Because of that, your theory is, of course, quite untenable. The few bombers still in commission are being used for more important operations. The bridges to the north of Liege must be destroyed at all costs."

"And those to the south, sir?"

"They must be kept intact so that our victorious troops can cross the Meuse."

"So you really believe that we'll get that far, sir?" I said, leaning forward in my chair.

"I can see nothing to prevent us," muttered the other softly, almost as though he were speaking to himself. "We've broken the back of any defence they can put up against us. It may take a little time, but I'm quite sure that there will be no retaliation on their part; or that if there is, it will be ineffective."

"I only wish I could feel as confident of that as you seem to be, sir."

The Commandant eyed me steadily for a long moment, a curious smile touching his thin lips. "I assure you, that it is a matter of fact," he said sharply. "Everything has been planned down to the last detail by no other person than the Feuhrer himself. Nothing will be allowed to deviate us from our course and we all have a part to play in that action. Our task will be, as before, the destruction of any enemy convoys moving up in the direction of the front. If enemy fighters are encountered, then it is your duty to destroy them too. Anything which will reduce the enemy's capacity for giving battle must be our target.'

I sat quite still in my chair. The other's strange and unbending faith in the Feuhrer seemed oddly pathetic and out of place. It was true that the attack on the ground was going ahead rapidly and we had achieved a momentous success, that the enemy were, at the moment, reeling back before the unexpected onslaught; but beyond that, I felt it foolish to commit oneself. The attack had come several months too late to be really effective, unless a miracle happened; and that was something I could not foresee. If we had hit the enemy as hard as this, and as decisively, the moment they had hit the beaches of Normandy, there would have been a chance that we could have succeeded in throwing them back into the sea. But not now.

They had a tremendous reserve of manpower and the air forces of the Allies were overwhelmingly superior in both numbers and quality of machines to ours. Their factories were working incessantly at full production, replacing their losses almost before they had been incurred. Whereas our plants had been bombed and gutted by fire, our rail communications were in a complete shambles and it was virtually impossible to move anything by road for fear of attack by the R.A.F. or the U.S.A.A.F.

I wondered vaguely whether the Commandant was so much of a fanatic that he had blinded himself to the obvious. If so, I felt instinctively, that he had a tremendous shock in store once the Allies regained the initiative—as I felt they were bound to do once they had received their poise and balance and had shortened their line.

"You think I'm wrong." I grew aware that the Commandant was looking directly at me. I felt myself flush slightly, then lifted my head. I hadn't been aware that my feelings had shown so clearly on my features.

"I'm not sure, sir," I said harshly. "It's just that I've an idea the enemy aren't quite as—"

The shrill wail of a warning siren in the near distance cut off the rest of the sentence. I caught a glimpse of the look of incredulous disbelief on the other's face as he started to his feet, his chair scraping back on the floor. The cigarette, still twisted into the holder, dropped from his hands into the tray as he walked swiftly around the desk and almost ran towards the door.

In spite of myself, I felt the surprise and the tenseness of apprehensive fear run through me as I pulled myself to my feet. It just didn't seem possible. The airfield had escaped the attention of enemy planes for so long now, that it had become almost an accepted fact that we were somehow, miraculously immune from air attack. Savagely, I choked down the rising feeling of futile anger. Oh God, what bloody fools we had been. We ought to have realised that the enemy might try something like this. They would have put two and two together and reasoned, quite naturally, that these fighters which had been knocking hell out of their convoys for the past few days, must have been operating from an airfield somewhere in the vicinity and it wouldn't have taken them long to locate us. The surprising thing was that they hadn't done it long before.

Possibly we had been deluding ourselves all the way down the line, falsely believing that we were safe from attack, that they would never notice us there, such a small place with such a small force of fighters, even though we were close to the front line.

I cursed myself bitterly for not having taken the possibility into account before. A five-year-old child ought to have seen through the enemy's plan. Mentally, I cursed myself again and again as I stumbled towards the door a split second behind Jensen and the Commandant.

There was no doubt that we had been caught on the wrong foot. The enemy planes were not yet in sight and it was impossible to estimate how much time we had in hand before they arrived over the airfield, but I felt sure that there would not be enough time to fly off any aircraft. Strangely enough, the thought that, perhaps, we were not their target, never entered my mind.

I ran outside desperately, straining my ears to pick up the sound of aero engines, but there was nothing. The siren wailed into silence, the last dismal note hanging on the air for several seconds before fading, as though the ears, tuned to its saw-edged howl, continued hearing it long after the actual sound had faded.

Seconds later, there came the sound of gunfire far to the south. It was impossible to make out anything through the patches of cloud, but the gunfire told its own tale. The anti-aircraft crews situated on the outskirts of the town, some three miles away, had picked up the enemy planes and had opened fire on them.

How effective this fire would be, it was difficult to tell. It would certainly not account for many of the enemy planes, but it told us two things instantly. Two important things. It gave us the direction from which the planes were approaching and it told us more definitely than anything else that it would be sheer suicide to try to get any planes into the air before the bombers were upon us. Three minutes. At the most, we had three minutes and even if one fighter did manage to take off within that time—and it was highly likely that they were all refuelled and ammunitioned ready for immediate take-off—it would be impossible for the pilot to climb to any height before the enemy bombers put in an appearance.

"What do you make of it, sir?" Jensen turned to the Commandant, his face twisted with indecision.

"Trouble." The other's voice was quiet, but certain. He seemed to have regained his composure rapidly. "This has never happened before, but I suppose we ought to have expected it. We can't expect to lead a charmed life all of the time. Sooner or later, they would have got round to us."

"We don't stand a chance in hell of getting any planes into the air in time to be effective."

"I realise that." I saw the Commandant clench his hands spasmodically by his sides, white-knuckled with the nervous pressure he was exerting.

"Here they come. From the east."

"From the east!" Jensen sounded incredulous.

"They must have circled around us, hoping to take us completely by surprise."

I listened, ears straining intently, and caught the intermittent thundering of the heavy engines a moment later. What the other had said was true. The enemy bombers were heading in from the east. Once again, they had outwitted us.

Less than a minute later, the first wave of them thundered overhead, bursting out of the cloud cover for a brief second before vanishing again on the far side of the airfield. Again, the thunderous roar of the engines dwindled to a fading murmur as the planes flew overhead, then began to bank steeply.

"Now they know where we are," muttered Jensen grimly. "They're turning back onto their bombing run."

"Get under cover! Quickly!" The Commandant was shouting the warning urgently at the top of his voice.

With a suddenness that blacked all thought in my head, the planes began to return. The desynchronised clamour of the powerful engines altered tone subtly, strengthened and deepened as they came in, this time from the northwest. Glimpsed only momentarily through rifts in the clouds, it was impossible to estimate how many of them there were, but to my startled gaze, there seemed to be more than a dozen of them, gigantic twin-engined shapes, roaring vengefully out of the clouds.

Jensen gave a hoarse cry and turned on his heel, running towards the concrete shelter on the far edge of the perimeter track. Realisation of the sudden danger struck at me with the violence of a physical shock. Madly, I took to my heels and followed him, stumbling on the wet grass. Then my feet were pounding on the concrete of the perimeter track and I flung myself forward, my heart pounding heavily in my throat, a painful tightness in my chest.

One after the other, we tumbled down the concrete steps into the damp darkness of the shelter. There was the sharp smell of decay and rotting leaves in my nostrils as

I crouched down beside Jensen. Someone else flung himself into the narrow opening and lay gasping violently for a moment, scarcely daring to move as the roar of the planes increased to an ear-shattering crescendo overhead.

"They mean business this time, "whispered the Commandant. In the dim light inside the shelter, his face seemed to possess an unnatural pallor, the skin stretched tightly across the bone structure of his face, only his eyes alive, deep-sunken, surrounded by tiny lines that gave him a gaunt appearance, a death's head, relieved only by the thin twitch of the bloodless lips as the high-pitched scream of falling bombs hammered at our ears.

Cautiously, I peered out of the opening, screwing up my eyes to make out the shapes of the incoming bombers. They came from the north-west, flying in line astern at about three hundred feet. As they dived over the airfield, they seemed to fan out as though each plane was searching for an individual target, although that was probably an illusory appearance brought about by shifting perspective.

But within seconds, it became increasingly obvious that they had one aim in view. The complete destruction of the airfield as a base of operations. They were flying strictly under orders as to what to destroy and what to leave untouched. A stick of bombs straddled the aircraft outside the hangar, bursting around and among them in a series of gigantic explosions.

Flames seemed to leap up out of the ground. There was a sense of unreality about the scene and I shook my head several times without seeming to move it. And yet this was reality, and I felt the fear beginning to stir in my mind again.

The sky around the oncoming bombers was curiously speckled and it took several seconds for me to realise that the guns right on the very edge of the airfield must have opened up. One of the planes had suddenly swung across my line of vision, dropping low over the further boundary marker. Then it levelled off, came in at less than fifty feet. More speckles appeared around it as every available gun on the battery site opened up. The element of surprise was gone. The planes now had to fly through an intense and lethal barrage of shells to get at the airfield.

The enemy bomber was almost over the outer perimeter track and I caught a glimpse of the bombs leaving the bomb bay and hurtling downwards towards the ground a split second before the entire plane disintegrated in a blinding sheet of flame.

The explosion sounded loud, even above the thunder of the exploding bombs as they fell along the runway. Behind the plane which had received the direct hit, a second bomber, streaking forward out of the clouds, swerved suddenly to starboard in an attempt to avoid the debris that was thrown almost another fifty feet into the air.

The bomb aimer must have pressed the release button at the same instant, for I saw the cluster of bombs fall from the belly of the plane; but it was a futile attempt. The sudden banking turn had thrown them violently off course and the stick of bombs landed in the fields to the west of the airfield, doing no damage.

But there were more to come. The enemy had evidently decided on no half measures as far as we were concerned. We had been a thorn in his side for long enough. This was to be the *coup de grace* as far as our squadron went.

The ground shuddered and heaved as more bombs landed. Out of the corner of my eye as I ducked my head, I caught a glimpse of the wall of the Control Block bulging outwards in a fantastic way, breaking up into individual jagged sections of brick and concrete, hurtling down to the ground, driven outwards by the terrible force of the stick of bombs which had obviously crashed through the roof and exploded inside.

"God help any of the poor devils who were inside there," said Jensen in a hushed voice.

He held himself stiffly against the wall of the shelter and there was a look of horror in his eyes. On the opposite side of the shelter, the Commandant pushed himself upright and came staggering forward, his face haggard and grey.

"What's happening?" he muttered hoarsely.

"The Control Block," I said, my voice almost drowned by the thunderous explosion nearby. Bits of concrete fell from the curved roof of the shelter onto our heads as we crouched down tensely, holding our breath. Dry-mouthed, feeling the sudden chill inside my body, I crouched against the hardness of the concrete wall and tried to shut out all sound. But even though I clamped my hands tightly over my ears, it still got through into my brain.

CHAPTER XI

The Long Retreat

The rising thunder of powerful engines was a huge noise, slamming hard at my ringing ears, biting deep into my terrified brain. I felt more afraid at that moment, than ever before. This was something I could not fight against; we were helpless, unable to do anything to help ourselves. More bombs came down. Thin, high-pitched whistles which temporarily blotted out even the sound of the planes roaring overhead. Then the bone-shaking explosions which terminated the shrieks of the falling bombs. Little thoughts ran aimless and senselessly through my brain.

My whole being seemed to have been torn down the middle by the concussive roar. I seemed to be suspended inside a bubble of agony but in spite of the pain, I knew that I had to pull myself together, that so long as we remained in the shelter we were safe from everything but a direct hit.

The smoke from the wreck and burning planes less than forty yards away rose up in a wide curtain that restricted my view, mingling with the low clouds overhead. Gradually, some of the terrible numbness in my body went away and I found myself able to think clearly for the first time since I had tumbled into the shelter. My brain began to tick over smoothly and quickly.

The last two bombers came in together, flying almost wing-tip to wing-tip, roaring low over the airfield. The guns in the distance had stopped firing and I could only surmise that they had been put out of action, possibly by a lucky hit. Fascinated, I watched them come in, unable to tear my gaze away from them.

They seemed to be coming directly at us and seconds later, there was a terrible scream as the bombs began to fall, closer this time than before. Fear almost choked me as I flung myself down with a hoarse, warning cry. I felt someone stumble against me and then everything outside seemed to erupt in a shower of smoke and flame-shot debris. A gigantic explosion shook the ground; a sound that could scarcely be heard because of ears deafened by the noise which had gone before.

Perhaps it was an indication of its nearness, the fact that I could scarcely hear it. Perhaps it was the vicious hammer-blow of the blast, sweeping in at the narrow opening, that clutched me around the middle and hurled me back against the inner wall of the shelter. Painfully, I hoisted myself to my feet, shook my head in an effort to clear it of the cordite fumes that filled everything, going down into my heaving lungs, choking me. My brain seemed filled with a dazed confusion left by the concussion of the bomb exploding less than ten yards from the entrance of the shelter.

The shock of the explosion had thrown me several feet, lifting me bodily, slamming me with an almost bone-breaking force against the concrete.

Steadying myself against the wall, clutching at it with both hands for support, I hung on for several seconds, trying to think clearly. My vision was blurred and details wavered insanely in front of my brimming eyes, behind a wall of tears that threatened to blind me temporarily.

Someone was moaning with a terrible intensity a few feet away in the smoke-filled darkness, but even though I turned my head slowly and tried to force my eyes to remain open, I could see nothing.

A lancing agony was the first conscious sensation of which I was aware. The pain jarred along my right arm where I had hit the rough surface of the concrete wall, up into my shoulder until I was forced to grit my teeth tightly together in my mouth to prevent myself from moaning out aloud with the biting agony.

At vague intervals, the darkness inside the smoke-filled shelter seemed less complete and I thought I could pick out vague shapes that moved and stumbled forward. For a long moment, however, my consciousness threatened to leave me completely and I tried desperately to remain on my feet, clutching frantically at the wall as my body began to slide downwards to the floor, my legs buckling beneath me. I was shaking violently and uncontrollably.

There was the acrid, choking stench of dust and smoke in my nostrils. Shaking my head numbly, I moved forward, feeling in front of me with my outstretched arms. There was a slick feeling of blood on my shoulder and I could feel it trickling down my right arm which hung almost uselessly by my side. Experimentally, I tried to move it, but every tiny motion sent a fresh wave of pain jarring along it.

With an effort, I forced down the feeling of sickness in the pit of my stomach and tried to thrust away the pounding, nauseous ache at the back of my eyes. The dust was settling slowly and I was able to see more clearly. Outside, there was a deep and almost terrifying silence. The thunder of aero engines had faded into the distance and the enemy bombers had left after fulfilling their mission of vengeance.

Swaying groggily on my feet for an instant, I took a couple of hesitant steps forward, felt something soft and yielding under my feet and paused, then went down on one knee and turned the body over with my good hand. The moaning ceased for a moment and I heard the man suck in a deep, agonised breath. Bending, I tried to make out the smoke-blackened features, my first concern for the other.

The Commandant, was lying on his side close to the rough wall, his mouth hanging open and a thin trickle of blood oozing slowly down his dust-smeared cheek. His eyes were half-closed, but they opened as I felt along his body, trying to discover whether any bones were broken. He exhaled sharply in an agonised bleat of pain as I touched his back and I saw the sweat pop out on his forehead as I tried to move him. Then he screamed thinly and his head, half-raised, fell back with a dull, sickening thud onto the floor of the shelter.

There was a sudden chill in my body as I looked about

me helplessly. It would be impossible to lift the Commandant unaided, even if that was a wise thing to do in his present condition. His back seemed to have been injured, possibly by the blast, or by a flying fragment of concrete; and it might have been fatal to move him.

Leaving him lying there in the dust, I crawled forward into the dark interior of the shelter. Now that my ears had become attuned to the silence, I could just make out the faint crackling of flames from somewhere outside and a vague, confused shouting somewhere in the distance.

Jensen lay motionless and still a few feet away from the inert body of the Commandant. He lay face downwards and did not stir as I turned him over with a tremendous heave which almost jerked my arm out of its socket. There was no sign of blood on his uniform and I felt for his pulse, trying to ignore the pounding of my own heart against my ribs. Finally, I managed to detect it, still beating strongly. Giving a sigh of relief, I felt along the back of his head. The hair just above his neck was matted with blood and it was abundantly clear that he had been knocked unconscious when he had fallen back against the concrete.

There was obviously nothing I could do there for the injured men and stumbling to the entrance I staggered out, almost falling into the arms of the two orderlies who came running forward over the grass in answer to my shouts.

"Get an ambulance over here—quickly!" I gasped hoarsely. "It's urgent!"

One of the men turned and ran back across the perimeter track without pausing to ask any further questions. The other glanced down into the shelter.

"How many are down there, sir?"

"Three," I said breathlessly. My tongue seemed to move rustily in my mouth and my lips felt dry and cracked. There was a stabbing pain in my shoulder that moved across my chest every time I drew in a deep breath. "The Commandant's there—pretty badly injured I think. Don't try to move him until the doctor gets here. I think it's his back. Possibly broken, but I'm not sure "

"Oh God." The words sounded more like a prayer than

an oath. "And the others, sir?"

"They're not so badly hurt, I don't think. One has been knocked unconscious by the blast, possibly suffering from concussion. I couldn't bring him round and with my arm as it is, I couldn't move him by myself."

"Better get the doctor to take a look at that shoulder when he gets here, sir," said the other, an expression of concern on his thin, pinched features. "You look about all in yourself."

"I'll be all right," I said thickly. "The others are in a worse state than I am. Better see to them first."

Less than two minutes later, the ambulance appeared on the scene, skidding to a noisy halt less than three yards from the entrance to the shelter.

"Better get inside there, doctor," I ordered. "The Commandant and two other pilots."

"How bad is it?' asked the doctor as he came forward and stood for a moment staring down into the gaping darkness of the shelter.

"Pretty bad, especially where the Commandant's concerned. His back may be broken, I'm not sure. You'll have to be careful when you're moving him."

The other nodded briskly. "We'll be careful," he said tersely, then glanced down at my arm. "You look as though you could do with some medical treatment yourself. Better wait here until we get these men out, then go back with them in the ambulance."

I nodded wearily. Carefully, the doctor and one of the orderlies entered the shelter and vanished from sight. Standing outside, I looked about me. As an airfield, it had ceased to exist. One or two of the fighters had been left undamaged. The rest were almost total wrecks. A stick of bombs, accurately dropped, had burst among them where they were clustered together in front of the hangar which itself was heavily on fire and burning from end to end.

Two of the fire-tenders were already on the scene, pumping foam and water into the blazing wreckage, but it was painfully obvious that they could never hope to get that fire under control. All that now remained was to leave it to burn itself out and salvage as much as possible from the ruins.

Closer at hand, there was a vast crater blown out of the perimeter track less than ten yards away. This was the bomb which had caused all of the damage as far as we in the shelter had been concerned, I thought wearily. Another few yards and it would have been a direct hit. There would have been nothing of us and our mortal remains would have been buried under a pile of rubble.

Once more the tremor of fear worked its way through my body and an uncontrollable spasm of weakness hit my legs, so that I could scarcely stand upright. The orderly looked at me closely:

You all right, sir?" He laid his hand on my arm and peered into my face.

Wearily, I nodded my head. "Yes, I'm all right. I seem to have hit my shoulder pretty hard when I fell inside there."

I tried to grin, but I knew inwardly that it would be only a feeble travesty of a smile. "I got thrown across the shelter by the blast of that bomb, but the opposite wall seems to have got in my way."

There was a movement inside the opening and a moment later the orderly came out backwards, holding onto Jensen's ankles while the doctor emerged a second later, lifting the other's head. Ten seconds later, he had been placed on a stretcher inside the back of the ambulance. The doctor came over to me and I could tell by the expression on his face that something was wrong.

"You were right about the Commandant," he said tensely. "It is his back. I'm not sure at the moment how badly he's been injured, but I'm acting on the assumption that his back may be broken. I've given him a stiff dose of morphia and I think that has deadened the pain appreciably, but unfortunately, he's still conscious."

"Do you think you can get him out, doctor?"

"It isn't going to be easy, but we'll have a try. We'll take a stretcher in with us and try to lift him onto it. That's the only way, I'm afraid."

"And the other pilot. How is he?"

"Dead, I'm afraid. There doesn't seem to be a mark on him, but he's dead. Must have been killed instantly."

"But that isn't possible. Surely it couldn't have been the blast."

The other shrugged his shoulders weakly. "That's the only explanation I can give at the moment without a thorough examination. Blast can do peculiar things to the human body, you know. I've seen a man standing almost on top of a bomb when it exploded and he suffered nothing worse than severe shock, while a man twice that distance away, collapsed and died within seconds from internal injuries. Maybe that's what happened in this case.

"That bomb landed pretty close. The blast might have been transmitted through the concrete wall of the shelter, even through the ground. It could have been a chance-in-a-million that he was standing in the right spot where it could prove fatal."

I looked down at the huge crater which had been gouged out of the ground. My mind was still dazed and exhausted, unable to take things in clearly and it was almost by a process of mental association that I visualised the dead man lying inside the smoke-filled interior of the shelter behind the seemingly impregnable concrete walls.

I turned back to the doctor, but he had already moved away and was giving orders to the two orderlies in a low voice. A moment later, they both followed him into the shelter carrying a stretcher between them.

When they emerged again a few minutes later, they were carrying the still figure of the Commandant, his face grey in the light, glistening with sweat. His lips were moving spasmodically, but no sound seemed to be coming out.

As they lifted him into the back of the waiting ambulance, he was seized by a sudden paroxysm of coughing and his back arched tensely for a moment, his face tightening abruptly as the intense pain bit deeply through his drug-induced stupor, into his brain. It was doubtful whether any amount of morphia could have prevented him from feeling that agony, I thought weakly.

The doctor looked round at me. "You'd better get inside with them," he said sharply. "We'll take a look at that arm of yours over at the hospital. Fortunately, the building there seems to have suffered very little damage."

"They were only intending to put the airfield and planes out of commission." I said wearily as I pulled myself up into the ambulance, helped by one of the orderlies. "And by the look of things, they certainly succeeded. I doubt whether any more planes will ever fly off from here."

A moment later, the door was shut behind me and I seated myself on the side of the bed opposite the Commandant and Jensen. The driver let in the clutch and we moved off over the rough, uneven ground, the ambulance bumping and swaying every second, so that it was impossible to keep in one place and pain lanced through my arm as the motion of the vehicle flung me around in the back.

At the hospital, Jensen was taken into one of the wards so that he could be kept under observation. I followed one of the orderlies into the room at the end of the main ward and sat patiently while a dose of morphia was injected into my arm and my shoulder was dressed and bandaged.

The skin had been torn in several places and two ribs badly bruised, but apart from that, there was nothing seriously wrong.

The Commandant was taken into the operating theatre and we never saw him again. Later, we learned that his back had indeed been broken and that he had died the next morning.

CHAPTER XII

Air Assault

"A really brilliant move for us," I muttered bitterly. "Somebody in Berlin must have taken their time in thinking this one up for us."

Jensen shrugged his shoulders and hunched himself forward on the edge of his chair. He looked unhappy and disconcerted. His head was still bandaged and there was a touch of greyness to his face which gave him an unhealthy pallor.

I swore again, savagely, and then glanced up at him. He shook his head slowly, helplessly.

"There doesn't seem to be anything we can do about it," he said despairingly. "That order must have come from Berlin. "It's official."

"But don't they see what they're doing by pulling us back there. They're as good as admitting defeat, not only here in the air but on the ground too. Hell, it isn't much of a boost to our morale to get orders like this."

"They must have a reason for it somewhere, I suppose," muttered Jensen mechanically. "Although for the life of me, I can't see it at the moment. I know we lost almost all of the available planes, but surely we aren't as short of aircraft as that. If we are, then the sooner we sue for peace, the better. The Americans come over, bomb the airfield and destroy seven of our planes. We still have two in commission and it would take only another seven to put us back into operation again. Another two pilots are all we need." He spoke slowly, obviously ill at ease, sitting on the very edge of his chair as though expecting to have to rise suddenly, at a moment's notice.

"What about the new Commandant?" I asked. "Have you seen him? Can he do anything about it, take it up to a higher level in the hope of getting it countermanded, or even reconsidered?"

"There isn't much chance of that, I'm afraid. I've only had a short meeting with Commandant Henschel, but he doesn't seem to be the kind of man who would take kindly to us telling him how to run this airfield."

I lit a cigarette and inhaled angrily. "Damn it all, it won't be much of an airfield unless we get some more planes here."

Jensen shrugged his shoulders dejectedly, but said nothing. Sitting there, he stared out of the low window across the stretching flatness of the airfield, where men were still hard at work filling in the deep bomb craters and levelling the runway once more, obliterating the scars of the raid some ten days earlier.

Watching him, I knew instinctively what he was thinking. Many things had happened since the enemy bombers had put in their unexpected attack which had virtually wiped us out as a fighting unit. On the ground, some fifty miles to the west, the German Army was reeling back in the face of a series of powerful blows. The enemy had not been driven back to the Meuse as had been so confidently predicted by the Commandant and the German Commanders at the front.

The enemy had fallen back in a disorganised rout during the first day or so of the attack, but gradually, they had shortened and established their front line, taken up a firm stand against our advance and brought up fresh reserves from the rear. They had recovered with a suddenness which had been both shocking and surprising. Here and there, although totally surrounded, they had fought tenaciously to cling to their forward outposts, stemming the tide of our advance so that we had been forced to thrust around them, removing troops from the front to deal with them, troops which we could ill-afford.

Then, inevitably, our advance had ground to a halt in the face of determined and stubborn resistance. The forward spearheads had come within sight of the Meuse only to be hurled back by superior forces. Our troops were tired men. They had advanced through the enemy's defensive line, breaching it in many places on a wide front. Had luck been with them, they would undoubtedly have won through. As it was, they had failed by the shortest possible margin.

As for ourselves, it had been a period of stagnation. Without planes, with our store of petrol and ammunition destroyed during the raid, we could do nothing. To have sent out the two remaining planes by themselves would have been asking for trouble. Such a mission would have been suicidal for the pilots and it was doubtful whether either of them would have returned from the first attack. The weather had cleared slightly during the past week or so. The air had become frostily clear with high clouds and little cover; and American fighters and bombers had become increasingly active in the vicinity of the battle front.

Jensen stirred himself suddenly, flicked away the stub of his cigarette and rubbed the muscles of the back of his neck. "Perhaps it won't be too bad, moving back to Berlin," he said slowly, screwing up his mouth. "It will mean, after all, that we're going back to our original function. That of defending the city against their bombers."

"It's still a retrograde step," I insisted. "Here, we were on the offensive, taking the battle to the enemy. Back in Berlin, we'll be simply waiting for them to come to us."

Jensen wavered. "Well, I'll have another talk with the

new Commandant as soon as possible, although I doubt whether it will do any good." He lit another cigarette and inhaled deeply. "As a matter of fact, he's asked us to go to see him this afternoon. No doubt, he wants to discuss the situation with us personally."

"Do you know anything about him, sir?"

Jensen shook his head. "Nothing much."

"I see."

"He isn't an aircrew man at all. Spent most of his life on the ground as far as I've been able to discover. It's a pity because you can't expect a man like that to be able to see things from our point of view. There must always be two schools of thought in the Luftwaffe. That of the men on the ground, and the opposing view of the men in the air. I doubt whether these view points can ever be really reconciled."

"He might see eye to eye with us if we put our case strongly enough." I tried to keep the bitterness out of my voice, but only partially succeeded. "With the army pulling back all along the front, you'd think they would need our support far more now than before."

"Somehow, in Berlin, they don't seemed to look at it that way. Either that, or they consider that our past experience has proved to be far more costly than they had anticipated and they don't think they can continue losing men and planes at this rate."

I shrugged. "That isn't much of an argument," I said sarcastically. "We had nothing to do with that raid. It did all of this damage they're so concerned about and we were simply unlucky there. It could have happened to anyone."

"But it happened to us," said Jensen heavily, "and as far as the powers that be are concerned, that's all there is to it."

"Then they're fools," I said harshly, getting to my feet. I walked over to the window and stood looking out, my hands thrust deeply into my pockets, trying to keep my anger in check. "I tell you, sir, if they once throw away this chance, and lose the battle of the Ardennes, then Germany is finished. Another six months at the most and the British and Americans will be hammering at the gates of Berlin, if the Russians don't get there first."

I paced the room angrily. I felt both concerned and shocked by the news, angry at myself too because of the feeling, deep down inside, that we had been unjustly treated. Because of something which had been completely outside of our control, we were being relegated to a rear position. Damn it all, I thought savagely, bitterly, if we had only received the warning of the approach of the enemy bombers two minutes earlier, we might have been able to fly off the entire squadron, and then the tables would have been turned with a vengeance. We would have held the whip hand and all this would never have happened.

It seemed only logical that we should remain here, that reinforcements should be sent as soon as possible and we should be ready to provide air cover for the retreating troops. During the short time we had been stationed there, we had grown to know the ground intimately. We knew the whereabouts of the enemy forward batteries and although they would be advanced or pulled back a few miles as the fighting front fluctuated back and forth, we would still possess the advantage over the enemy.

We knew how to make ourselves invisible from the enemy gunners. We knew where the hills lay, rising clear of the flat ground, ready to reach up and snatch down the unwary pilot, leaving him in a pile of blazing wreckage on some bare hillside.

Yes, I thought bitterly, that was where my anger originated and although I tried desperately to stifle it, to think clearly and logically, it was slow to go away.

"Perhaps they have made a grievous mistake in ordering us back right away," admitted Jensen, "and we ought to put it to the Commandant when we see him. But we've got to look at the long-term position. If the enemy continue to advance at their present rate, they will have recaptured all of the ground they lost during our offensive, and within a few weeks at the most, they will be here. We'll have to pull back then."

"Of course." I leaned against the wall and stared moodily through the window. The two planes still stood in front of the twisted structure of the destroyed hangar. In a way they seemed to symbolise the futility of all we were trying to do. How could anyone expect us to fight against an enemy like this, who could take the most devastating blow we could deliver and still come back fighting savagely? For a moment, I felt as though I had made a complete fool of myself.

"Let's see what the Commandant has to say about things first," said Jensen soothingly. "There's no point in crossing our bridges until we come to them." He paused, then looked up at me as though a new thought had just struck him. "How are the rest of the men taking the news? You seem to be more in touch with them than I am."

I blinked at the suddenness of the question, then recovered. "They seem to be taking it all right, I suppose." I hesitated. "They seemed to be a lot better a few days ago, before that raid made a mess of everything. But there does seem to be something different about them. It isn't lack of sleep any more, you realise that. It's something else. As though they've lost all interest in their work."

I shook my head slowly, wondering how to put my thoughts into words. It was very difficult. "There's nothing mutinous about their actions. They don't go talking out of turn as I did a few minutes ago, but you can see it in their eyes if you look close enough. You can see that they don't know what they're supposed to do now, that they think everything is finished as far as the war and Germany are concerned.

"It was different when we first arrived here. Then they were all out on their feet, they couldn't think straight, they were too damned tired to really know what they were doing, but they went up in those planes and they fought it out with the enemy. They had something concrete to do then and there was the feeling that things were going a lot better for us, that for the first time since the enemy invaded Europe, we had a chance to turn the tide and throw them back into the sea, and that their little effort was worthwhile, that they were doing something about it in their own small way. It was how I felt, possibly how you felt yourself, so I think you can imagine their feelings when they're suddenly told that they're not wanted here any longer, that they're to go back, right away from the fighting zone, back to Berlin, to take over a defensive role again. It's a little too much to take in fully all at once."

Jensen looked at me for a long moment, then nodded his head and said very gently. "We're all expendable. That's one thing we must realise from the very beginning. We receive orders and we're supposed to obey them without question."

"I realise that, sir. But it isn't easy to impress it on the others when you can't see the reason for it yourself. They've changed completely. Now they're apathetic, utterly indifferent to what goes on around them. Hopeless and lost, that's my opinion for what it's worth."

"We'll see the Commandant," said the other, rising to his feet. "If he can do anything about it, there may be a chance. If not, then we go back to Berlin within the next two days."

* * * *

"I thought I'd better get you all together at the first opportunity," began the Commandant thinly. He surveyed us all over his rimless spectacles, moving his head jerkily as though trying to take everyone in in a single glance. "As you know by now, the position of the fighter group based here has altered considerably since the—ah, unfortunate—incident ten days ago."

He paused and glanced about him, a grim expression on his face. Commandant Henschel was a small, thin-faced man who held himself very erect in his chair, his back stiff as a ramrod, his head held high. A man with a big inferiority complex, I thought reflectively, watching him closely from beneath lowered lids. A dangerous man to cross. I doubted whether we would get much satisfaction from him.

"We no longer have the necessary facilities for keeping a fighter squadron on the station and—" He held up his hand as Jensen half rose in his chair and made as if to speak. "I know what you want to say, but you'll have your chance in a few moments. Firstly, I'd like to put my position to you.

"The raid which destroyed most of the planes based here, did far more than that. It showed that without an adequate warning system we're far too susceptible to a surprise attack. It was clearly impossible for us to get any planes into the air to meet this bomber attack. Had that been possible, the picture would have been drastically different. The enemy might have been caught on the wrong foot and possibly most of that bomber force could have been destroyed before it had a chance to press home its attack. The fact that it could come in unopposed, meant that they could virtually pick their targets and do the maximum amount of damage without loss to themselves.

He paused a moment, his fingers resting lightly on the polished top of the desk. The ring on his right hand glinted brilliantly in tiny flashes in the sunlight that came streaming in through the window. His lips were compressed into a tight line and there were little shadows under his eyes as he allowed his gaze to fall upon each of us in turn.

Then he went on quietly: "The High Command in Berlin consider that there is no further need for a fighter squadron to be based here, so close to the enemy lines where it can come under surprise attack. Accordingly, they have—"

"No need!" said Jensen savagely. He was already on his feet, glaring angrily at the Commandant. "That's nonsense. Utter nonsense!"

The Commandant's face hardened. I noticed his fingers curling together on the top of the desk. He seemed to jerk back in his chair as though he had been physically struck in the face.

"What was that you said, Jensen?" he demanded. His voice was quiet and silky, ominous. His glance had whipped round and was fixed tautly on the other.

"I said it was utter nonsense," repeated Jensen distinctly. He held himself up very straight. "If there ever was need of a fighter squadron based here, that time is now. Less than fifty miles away, our troops are pulling back in the face of a tremendous onslaught. They need as much support as they can get. Our own bombers don't seem to be able to do anything to help them. Either we don't have any here, or they're too indispensable to use, in support of ground troops. But at least we could do something, destroy their convoys. We've got the speed and the manoeuvrability that the heavy bombers haven't. I say there ought to be a squadron based here to cover the strategic withdrawal of our troops."

"Somehow, I think you have things a little out of focus," said Henschel thinly. He seemed to be holding himself tightly under control with a supreme effort. His hands, white-knuckled, lay flat on the desk and his eyes were very angry. There was a deepening colour in his face, burning in two spots high on his cheeks.

Jensen lowered himself into his seat. He looked tired and dejected, as though the effort of that outburst had taken more out of him than he had anticipated.

"Within weeks, possibly within days, the Americans will have occupied Bitburg. This airfield will pass into their hands. That is something we have to face. Nothing we can do will prevent it. That is something which must always be taken into consideration, and I understand, is the over-riding reason behind these orders."

"But why Berlin, sir?" I asked, leaning forward. "Surely that will be merely relegating us into a defensive role once more. Couldn't they have pulled us back sufficiently to prevent the airfield where we were stationed from falling into enemy hands, and yet leaving us sufficiently close to the front to give our troops support?"

"Please," said Henschel carefully, his eyes gleaming with a faintly vindictive light, "please give the authorities in Berlin credit for knowing the best positions to place our fighter planes. After all, they can see the overall position, while you can know only one tiny corner of it. You can't possibly appraise the overall situation."

"I didn't mean it that way, sir," I said stiffly. "I simply mean that—"

"I realise quite well what was in your mind," went on the other quickly, holding up his hand. He got to his feet, stood for a moment behind the desk, then walked over to the nearby wall where the huge map of the whole country covered it almost entirely.

"Have any of you any idea of how the other battle is progressing?" he demanded thinly. His nasal voice reached every corner of the room. Slowly, he turned his head, then nodded, smiling faintly as though secretly pleased with himself.

"No. I thought not. Stationed out here, you see only what is happening on this particular front. But here, just to the east of Berlin, a far more dangerous battle is being fought, one on which the whole future of Germany may depend, whether or not we are conquered. You've been here for so long that you seem to have blinded yourself to the fact that Germany faces another and potentially a more dangerous enemy.

"Already, the Russian armies are thrusting forward through Poland towards our eastern borders. They are far closer to Berlin than either the British or the Americans. And the whole future of Germany as a nation will depend upon who gets there first."

He lowered his voice, went back and sat down in his chair. For the first time since I had seen him, I had the impression that he, too, was a tired and dispirited man; that he no longer believed in the invincible might of Germany.

Looking up, he said quietly. "The Americans and the British are soft-hearted fools. They fight us and try to persuade themselves that they will destroy us utterly, but that is not so. One must have a knowledge of these things, must know these people intimately, know why they fight, what ideals drive them on, and how their national characteristics will alter them once the war is finished. I tell you all, gentlemen, in all seriousness, that the war is already lost, but that if we have to submit, it must be to the Western Coalition and never to the Russians.

"They seek to destroy and dominate us utterly. The British and Americans will forget what has happened and ten years in the future, Germany will rise again, as strong as ever. But if the Russians capture Berlin, then that can never happen. Germany will be destroyed.

"That, I believe, is why you have been ordered to pull back to Berlin. There will be plenty of fighting for you there, have no fear of that." He paused, glanced down at Jensen and went on slowly. "A little while ago, I believe you were on the point of asking whether or not it would be possible to have these orders countermanded, or modified. Do you still wish to ask that now that you've heard the other side of the story?"

Jensen was silent for a long moment, sitting slumped in his chair, then he stirred as if he had only just heard the other's question. Giving a brief shake of his head, he said slowly:

"No, sir. I take back all of that. As you say, there are a lot of aspects about the military situation we don't know fully."

Henschel nodded, satisfied. "It's important that you should report for your new duties as soon as possible. You'll leave here tomorrow morning and take the train to Berlin. The journey won't be easy. The R.A.F. have bombed the railway system and it may not be possible to get through."

"I think we all realise the position, sir," said Jensen softly.

A moment later, Henschel rose to his feet to signify that the meeting was over. Going outside, I stood for a moment looking about me. There was a turbulence in my mind that I couldn't define. It was as though one chapter in my life had suddenly closed and another, dark and mysterious, was slowly beginning to open.

CHAPTER XIII

Fire Over Berlin

The airfield to which we had been assigned was less than ten miles from the eastern outskirts of Berlin. Here, the country was flat and wet and snow still lay on the ground, covering everything with a clinging, moist, white sheet. The clouds were lowering ominously, threatening, when we arrived after a nightmare journey which had taken us the best part of three days, stopping in sidings while the train in which we travelled was shunted back and forth onto the main line, taking wide detours to avoid the places with the most damage.

The journey had done more than try my patience. It had given me a horrified insight into the utter devastation which existed all over Germany. Everywhere, towns lay in ruins where the enemy's heavy bombers had blasted them without mercy. Sidings, marshalling yards and once-busy junctions had been blasted into a terrible shambles and it seemed incredible that the train was able to move at all.

Factories had been bombed into heaps of wreckage and it was becoming painfully obvious that the enemy were ranging over the whole of the country, virtually unopposed, bombing wherever they wished. The aftermath was terrible to witness. It was no wonder that our war effort had been reduced almost to zero.

As we had neared Berlin, the damage had become, if anything, worse than elsewhere. Scarcely a mile of railway track had been left undamaged. Wrecked trains, many of them loaded high with tanks and guns, stood in sidings, unable to move.

Beyond Berlin, however, to the east, things were a little better. It was almost as if the enemy had drawn a rigid demarcation line down some map at their Air Force Headquarters and given orders that nothing beyond that line was to be bombed. The Russians seemed to have made little attempt to bomb the area although it was common konwledge that they had several squadrons of planes, including heavy bombers, only a little distance behind their front line.

I broached this point with Jensen as we stood outside the long, black hangar and stared about us on that first day among our new surroundings.

"Perhaps they're holding them in reserve," he said thoughtfully, "hoping to be able to throw them in as a crushing *coup de grace* when we're least expecting it."

"But you think that the main attacks will still come from the west?"

Jensen nodded. "I'm sure of it. Knowing the Russians, as our friend Commandant Henschel would say, I can't see them wasting their planes bombing Berlin when they can leave it to the British and Americans to do it for them. The Russian leaders are no fools. They realise how important it is to the British and Americans to continue this round-the-clock bombing and they're determined not to use their men and aircraft unless it's absolutely necessary. When the war ends, I know which country will be the strongest."

"That's what I'm afraid of." I bit my lower lip. "The British I understand, to a lesser extent, the Americans. But the Russians are totally different. They don't even think in the same way as we do. There always seems to be something more at the back of their minds than they show on the surface."

We went into the billet to warm ourselves. Outside, the air was cold with a warning of more snow on the way and the knowledge that we would, in all probability, soon be in action again, did little to bring any comfort into my mind.

* * * *

The full moon was hanging low on the eastern horizon, surrounded by long, thin clouds, tipped with white that stood out against the star-filled sky like shavings of wood pulled back from the face of the moon. The engine coughed momentarily, then burst into roaring, full-throated life, making the cockpit shake and shudder with the bawling, rattling force of it.

Outside, through the cockpit, I saw the sergeant lift his right hand to indicate that everything was clear. The engine roared as I increased the feed, spun into a glassy disc. The instrument panel rattled and jumped in protest, then steadied and settled down to a continuous rattle that jarred a little on my raw nerves, then passed into a background noise which had no more effect on me.

Gently, I eased the plane forward, felt the first faint tremorings of fear in my brain, to be swiftly followed by the cold, icy calm which always came once things were under way and there was no time in which to think about what might lie ahead, time only to concentrate on the task in hand, to measure the present in terms of fractions of a second, when everything that counted, seemed compressed into such a short interval of time, that outside of it, nothing else existed in the whole world.

This time, however, things were different. A new station, a new plane, and a new enemy to face. The more I thought about it, the more my brain forced itself into a tightening web of panic, the tightness came back into my stomach and I found myself wondering whether this time, I might not survive, whether my luck, which had somehow held so far, might fail me and my last glimpse of earth would be through a rising curtain of petrol-exploded flame, my body crushed to pulp in the steel of the cockpit, folding like paper about my limbs. It had happened to others in the past, men I had known intimately, men I had flown with, laughed and joked with, eaten and worked with. Death was the great equaliser, and could come to anyone. Nobody was immune.

We had some new men flying with us now. Most of the

old hands were there in the flights, but the others were new pilots and in spite of everything, there was not the same degree of trust in them as there had been in the old ones.

How these men would react once they came within sight of the enemy bombers and had to fly forward in the face of concentrated, accurate fire, would remain to be seen. Deep down inside of me, there was always the fear that someone would panic and then all would be lost. Our lives and the success of our mission would depend upon the coolness and calm nerves of every man in the squadron.

The moon threw a long lane of faint silver over the runway as I swung the plane round at the end of it, waited my turn to take off. Automatically, I revved up the engines, listened instinctively to their comforting roar. The plane shook through its entire length.

On the controls, my fingers were dancing madly as the vibration passed up into them and then into my body. The voice of the airfield controller was speaking softly and calmly in my ears, murmuring tinnily in the headphones.

Only seconds later, I received the signal to take-off. The runway ahead of me was clear. The Messerschmitt rumbled along it, gathering speed, shaking furiously as the tyres clawed at the ground. A bomb crater, relic of some earlier raid, flashed by less than ten feet away in a blur of moon-thrown shadow. A fraction of a second later, I eased back the stick, felt the plane respond, the nose come up, and the undercarriage lifted smoothly, rising clear of the ground, the plane climbing smoothly, nosing its way up into the clear air.

The atmosphere at thirteen hundred feet was clean and bright and very clear. Scarcely any clouds were visible; the stars stood out in their thousands, keen and brilliant.

I could almost feel the plane sliding smoothly and effortlessly through this great, jet void, seeming to be without physical contact of any kind with the dark earth below. There was a strangely ethereal quality about the darkness as the sky moved around me, slid over the cockpit, above and below.

For one fleeting, curious moment, I had the unshakable impression that I could surrender myself entirely to this evanescent void, this stretching wilderness which had suddenly become every possible horizon, reaching out to every compass point; that I could lose myself entirely and become a part of it, with no contact at all for the earth and the things of the earth.

Then, abruptly, almost before I was aware of it, the sensation passed. Shaking my head slowly, I checked the instruments, then turned my head slowly from side to side, watching as the other planes came rising up out of the dark ground and swung south beside me on the first leg of the course which would take us west of Berlin, so that we might place ourselves on the route taken by the enemy bombers.

I sensed the sudden wariness inside my brain as I eased myself more comfortably in my seat. From now on, until we sighted the enemy, it was purely routine. The plane would almost fly itself. I shook my head in muddled irritation. This was a mood, and when flying like this, I didn't like to have such moods. For some peculiar reason, my mind seemed to be rusting up, my thoughts scraping their way along circuitous tracks instead of running straight and smoothly in my brain.

With a conscious physical and mental effort, I took a tight grip on myself and tried to inject a little logic and common sense into my fuddled mind. The thought of the enemy bombers lying somewhere ahead in the darkness, their paths due to intersect with ours as though fate were leading them to us, had upset my train of thought considerably in spite of everything I could do about it. My body felt oddly cold and stiff and I moved my legs experimentally, to ease the sharp, shooting pains of incipient cramp that threatened to knot my muscles and twist them into jangled balls of agony.

Often, during a waiting period such as this, when nothing seemed to be happening and there was plenty of time in which to look at the position objectively and ponder over the many facets and possibilities it presented, I felt a kind of depression settling upon me and there was the vague suspicion, gradually growing into a certainty, that there was no other possible world than this, and no other alternative existence for us but the eternal plod of war, the going out with the dusk, the seemingly endless combat with the enemy, and the returning to base with first light, if you were lucky.

An endless sucession of nights and days with no real meaning behind them, nothing concrete to hang on to; and on top of everything, conditioning my thoughts to a tremendous extent, filling them with the inescapable thought that my whole life would be nothing but a constant repetition of what had happened in the past, that the fighting and the continual danger were everlasting.

That other world which had seemed to exist such a long time before, endless years ago, somewhere in the dim past of memory, had been nothing more than a brief dream, a half-remembered shadow before the rising of the curtain on horror and fear and terror, the limitless panorama of the stunted imagination which could contain nothing more than flaming guns, lumbering bombers, flak rising up in a sheeted curtain from the dark ground, lit with fire so that it seemed that one was hovering over the very Pit of Hell itself, gazing down upon the souls in torment.

Confusion existed in my mind for a long moment and although I knew, instinctively, that I should not be thinking along these lines, I found myself unable to help it. Where was it all leading? This jumbled memory of thick clouds and moonlight, of death that stalked the upper air in the form of spitting cannon and machine-guns. A glittering scythe of bullets and blazing petrol; everything clouded over by the fog of fear. The fear of dying and the lesser fear that all of this would continue on into some dim and unguessable future which was limitless.

At such times as that, reason vanishes; the thought that even if by some miracle we were to escape death during the whole course of the war, we would do so only to die in some concentration camp in Siberia, never occurred to me. I thought back to those who had already died while I had been with the squadron. Albrecht, Eberbach and the others. There was a numbing feeling of horror in my mind as I realised that although they had been dead for only a few weeks, already, I was finding it difficult to remember their faces. Their memory was fading swiftly. Soon, they would be all but forgotten, remembered at times whenever anyone recalled their names, but completely lost otherwise.

The thought frightened me more than I had ever thought

possible. For these men, as for a great many, the end of everything had come without the assurance that the world they had known such a long time before, could ever exist again, even if only for a brief period.

I felt a shiver run through me and my fingers tightened convulsively on the controls. It was gradually becoming more and more difficult, sitting there in the middle of it all, to believe that both of these worlds, those of peace and war, so utterly different and divorced from each other, could ever be reconciled. The historians would attempt to fit them together, slotting them into each other in some manner known only to themselves, striving to make logic out of all of this insanity.

It was at times such as this, that one tried to look for the miracle which could make it all come true. Many never discovered it, for it remained only in their memories, held onto and cherished with all the strength and might of the mind. I myself, after seeing the state in which the country now lay, had no doubt whatever that the war would end very soon; that we would be defeated. But what would come after that? Certainly not the brave new world promised by Hitler in the balmy days before the war when Germany had seemed to rise triumphant over all other countries of the world.

No, that wasn't the answer, I thought wearily. These promises had been made many times in the past and they had never been fulfilled. Always, there had been some new war, following close on the heels of that which had gone before. History had always repeated itself far too monotonously for any faith to be placed in miracles. I felt the black mood of depression sweep through me once again in an irresistible wave.

You didn't know exactly what you were supposed to be fighting for; you knew even less what you were dying for. In all this world of terror and violence, what was there for men such as us that was real and lasting?

The truth of it all was, I reflected wearily, that the world could no longer subsist without war. It had been going on for centuries and there was no new way it could find of an annihilation that destroyed several million of the world's inhabitants and decimated the cities and towns.

I leaned back in the seat, felt it hard against my

shoulders. Slowly, the hands of my watch ticked themselves around the circular face. Each minute seemed to
have suddenly lengthened itself in some peculiar way so
that the seconds were long, terrible things, and minutes
seemed like hours to my taut nerves.

Inside the cramped cockpit, it was still cold and stuffy.
Down below, the flooding moonlight touched the clouds
which had suddenly appeared off the port bow, turning
them into fluffy patches of white that stood out stark
and clear against the blackness of the night.

They drifted aft as we climbed a little, turning slightly;
and then blended together somewhere behind the tail.
Watching them, I felt as if my sense of time and motion
had been destroyed. Up here in the air, such mundane
things appeared to move so slowly and with an utter
absence of sound that could scarcely be comprehended.

It was as though nothing that was human could ever
destroy the peaceful serenity that existed here, not even
our own noisy, thunderous presence which was, after all,
only a very temporary thing.

Gently, I eased my tight-fisted hold on the control
column and forced myself to relax. There was no sense
in getting myself wound up so tightly that, when the time
came for quick thinking and instant action, I would be
unable to respond. We turned in unison, onto a new course
which would eventually bring up Berlin on our starboard
bow, some fifteen miles away.

My eyelids were twitching uncontrollably and there was
an uncomfortable prickling of the small hairs on the back
of my neck. Inwardly, I felt very tired and I could feel
the strain settling in the muscles of my face, pulling it
into a tight and ugly mask beneath the helmet. There
were times when the monotonous drone of the engine
brought on an unutterable sense of weariness and the long,
dragging minutes of forced concentration swarmed over
me like a feeling of hypnosis.

"It looks as though there's something over there. Starboard thirty." Rundstein's voice broke in upon my
thoughts and I jerked up savagely, aware that I had
almost fallen asleep.

"Where? Are you sure?" Jensen's tone was urgent.

"About thirty of them, sir. Closing rapidly. I'd say

they were on a collision course with us."

"I don't see anything. Are you sure?"

"I see them too," I said quickly as I caught a glimpse of the formation of tiny black dots, just visible for a brief moment against a patch of white cloud. An instant later, they had vanished again as they moved on into the blackness of the surrounding night sky. But that one look had been sufficient to confirm Rundstein's observation.

"All right," Jensen said quietly, never doubting us for a moment after I had spoken, "keep your eyes open. They may have brought a fighter escort along with them this time. There's just the possibility that they're operating their fighters from airfields in France."

We closed rapidly with the enemy formation. As we approached, I was able to make out the shapes of the individual planes. There were almost a hundred of them, I realised with a sense of milk shock. In the darkness, it had been impossible to make an acurate estimate of their numbers from five or six miles away. Now I saw that what I had taken for the complete formation when they had slid across the cloud bank, had in reality, been simply a small portion of them. The rest had been invisible against the pitch darkness.

Jensen had them spotted now. His voice came quietly over the intercom. "Take up attacking positions. We'll go in from seven thousand feet, astern. Pick your targets and act individually. No sign of fighter escort so far."

Peering forward, I lifted my gaze and squinted up into the dark heavens above the enemy formation now less than a mile away. The sky seemed clear of fighters, but that was nothing to go by. There was no way of telling at what height they would be flying. It was possible that they were up thereat close on ten thousand feet, keeping out of sight, tucking themselves away where it would be difficult for us to spot them until it was too late.

The glare of the moonlight on the outer surface of the cockpit canopy, diffracted into a diffuse glow as it was transmitted through the plastic, reflected many times internally, almost blinded me and I glanced down swiftly again, blinking my eyes several times.

Swiftly, I swung into a tight turn and fed more power to the engine. It responded instantly and I climbed in a shallow sweep, taking up the prescribed position behind the enemy bombers. So far, they had given no indication of knowing our presence there, either by opening fire or altering course.

I smiled grimly to myself. That could be one of the oldest tricks in the book they were playing. They would know that we had the edge on them as far as speed and manoeuvrability were concerned, so they would play dead until we came within range of them and then open up with everything they had. If we attacked without suspecting anything like this, there was a reasonable chance that they would have the initiative and that we would find ourselves caught in a vicious, murderous crossfire from which there was no escape.

I held myself under tight control. To go hurtling down upon the enemy, to satisfy the flaming, primitive lust for action, was my first impulse. With an effort, I withheld the urge. There was just the chance that this was what the enemy wanted us to do. They seemed to be remarkably unconcerned about our presence, although it seemed hardly likely that of all the men in that armada, not one of them had spotted us. That was, perhaps, the most essential task of the gunners and pilots when they were on the run in to the target but still several miles away.

Acting on impulse, I lifted the nose of the Messerschmitt and climbed steeply for several hundred feet, screwing up my eyes against the glare of the moonlight, scanning the dark sky above me. A moment later, I saw them; small, dark shapes, occasionally lit by the moonlight flashing off their wings. From that distance, it was impossible to identify them exactly, but there was no doubt in my mind what they were.

British fighters, flying above us, some two or three thousand feet higher than we were. I felt a sudden feeling of dismay blended with savage anger surge through me as I hit the transmitting button.

"Enemy fighters directly overhead, diving out of the moon."

My skin prickled uncomfortably, but with an effort, I forced myself to keep calm and settled my body deeper into the seat. There was only one thing to do now, in the circumstances, and I did it instinctively. The bombers would have to be left to their own devices for the moment. No danger could be anticipated from that quarter. The immediate danger, and it was a very real one, came from above.

Desperately, I continued the climb, banking steeply to starboard, only dimly aware that the other fighters had picked up my warning and were taking swift, evasive action. Something winked into a sphere of expanding light at the corner of my vision, dangerously close. I turned my head sharply, attracted by it in spite of the tight grip I had clamped on my actions.

The flash was a shell exploding just outside the canopy. The plane shuddered with the force of the explosion, lurched madly and before I was aware of it, the starboard wing-tip had gone and the plane was losing height rapidly.

CHAPTER XIV
Against All Odds

The next few moments were among the most unpleasant I had ever spent. Despite the fact that there had been no direct hit on the plane, I knew instinctively that unless I pulled it out of this dive, there would be no hope for me. Savagely, I pulled back on the stick, fighting for control. The plane was turning slowly about its longitudinal axis as it spun towards the ground. There was the thin, high-pitched scream of air rushing past the nose and cockpit, sounding even above the thunderous roar of the engine.

For what seemed an eternity, the plane refused to respond to the controls. Everything seemed to have dissolved into a blur of moonlight and stars and darkness, all streaming across my distorted vision in whirling lines of fire. Then, slowly, painfully slowly, she came back onto an even, diving motion, still losing height dangerously quickly, but the whirling of moon and star images steadied and then ceased in front of my eyes.

Using all of my strength, I tugged back on the control column, breathing heavily, feeling the air gushing out of my lungs with the tremendous, unaccustomed effort. It took the best part of fifteen seconds to bring the nose up, slowly but surely. Not until I was flying on an even keel did I allow myself to breathe easily.

The altimeter showed fifteen hundred feet. It was now well below the bomber force and far below the level of the fighter umbrella. Satisfied that the plane was now responding satisfactorily, I began to climb again, eyes alert for the first sign of the enemy. At the corner of my vision, something fell blazing out of the sky, dragging a long trail of fiery smoke behind it. Another followed a moment later and over the edge of the cockpit, I saw the first plane strike a hump of ground in the distance, the trail of burning wreckage smeared for half a mile down the hillside.

The sliding shapes above me, when I finally spotted them, were difficult to analyse. Desperately, I tried to identify the enemy. The fighting seemed to have broken up into snarling dog-fights all over the sky. Machine against machine, pilot against pilot.

My train of thought stopped abruptly. A dark shape slid across my sights and I recognised it instantly. A Hurricane, one of the fighters, diving down swiftly, trying to set himself up on the tail of one of the Messerschmitts. I turned swiftly, instinctively, cursing softly to myself as the dark shape slid tantalisingly away from the sights. The other pilot had grown aware of my presence, had forgotten his original intention and was only intent on shaking himself free of me.

I fired a short burst, saw the glint of tracer pass beneath his wing-tip, corrected swiftly, and kept my fire on the firing button for the best part of twenty seconds. Even in the darkness, it was possible to see the cannon shells lacing into him, stitching themselves into the sleek fuselage, being swallowed by the plane. Bringing up the nose of the Messerschmitt, I flew less than twenty feet above the Hurricane, saw the burst of smoke that trailed out from almost immediately behind the cockpit. Seconds later, there was a brilliant red flash which was transmitted into a streamer of fire as the enemy plane broke up in mid-air, pieces of debris whirling away in all directions.

For the next hour, we played cat and mouse with the British fighter escort. Unable to concentrate any of our attention on the bomber force, they inevitably got through.

By the time the enemy fighters broke off the engagements and flew away to the south-west, we were virtually out of petrol and ammunition.

In the distance, a vague, overall ruddy glow stained the clouds and almost blotted out the light of the moon. Berlin was burning. The enemy, opposed only by the anti-aircraft guns on the outskirts, had pressed home their attack with their usual determination. The Lancaster bombers had delivered their tremendous bomb load among the railway sidings, marshalling yards and in the industrial area.

I looked at the spreading red blaze numbly and felt a surge of bitter frustration pass through me. My brain felt empty and tired. It had been our task to prevent the enemy bombers from getting through, to destroy as many as possible on the way in and leave the few which remained, scattered and demoralised, to the mercy of the guns. But once again, we had been caught on the wrong foot. The presence of the Hurricanes was something we had not allowed for; and yet it was something we ought to have allowed for.

I felt the bitter taste of chagrin in my mouth as I pulled the plane round on course and joined formation with the others. We were fools, I told myself savagely, thinking that the enemy would send such a force of heavy bombers into the heart of the Reich, unescorted, when they had a host of new airfields in France and the Low Countries from which to fly off their fighters.

It was no excuse to say that this was the first time we had ever known it. It was the duty of a fighter pilot to be prepared for every conceivable eventuality. With an effort, I swallowed thickly, felt a shudder run through my body as I thought of the hundreds of men and women and children who had been killed in that holocaust of bombs which had fallen on Berlin, most of it because of our own blind stupidity.

In vain, I tried to tell myself that it wasn't fair to lay all of the blame for this upon ourselves. Even if we had known that the fighters would have been there, there would have been little else we could have done, other than what we did. To have gone for the bombers instead of the fighters would have been suicidal. Had that happened, we would have been wiped out almost to a man and the bombers would have got through to their target anyway after the escorting fighters had dealt with us.

It was still dark, with the moon standing high in the south-west when we finally came in to land. The runway was clearly visible even without the lights. Mechanically, almost without thinking, I touched down, felt the wheels bump on the concrete, held the plane steady along the stretching length of the runway and taxied around the perimeter track.

There was a chill coldness in the air as I climbed down and stood for a moment, gulping fresh air into my lungs.

Jensen joined me a few moments later. His face was pale and grim. He had taken off his helmet and was holding it absently in his right hand.

Falling into step with me, he said tightly: "We lost three planes altogether. Rundstein says he's sure the pilot of one of them baled out before it hit the ground, but we'll just have to wait and see as far as the others are concerned."

"We didn't make much of a showing tonight, did we?" I said bitterly.

He shook his head slowly. "That was something I only half-expected. It's never happened before to the best of my knowledge. It was fortunate that you spotted them when you did or their trick would have come off. We played right into their hands going straight for the bombers like that."

"They kept well above the Lancasters. Maybe it was instinct that made me look up. But the bombers must have seen us. In that brilliant moonlight it would have been impossible not to have spotted us and yet they made no move to open fire on us or break formation. There had to be something around for them to have been as confident as that. Usually they're so jittery that they break away as soon as we get with half a mile of them."

"They're no fools—we know that now, to our cost, perhaps," conceded the other.

Our footsteps crunched in companionable unison on the rough gravel of the perimeter track as we made our way back to our billets. The snow was still threatening and in the east, the clouds were beginning to gather, blotting out the brilliant stars. The air was bitterly cold, threatening to freeze the blood in my veins, stiffening my legs and arms.

My brain was humming with reaction and there was that exquisite, fine-drawn sensation of agony, like a massing of tiny pressures behind my skull that was not quite unbearable, with every cell of my brain seemingly stretched to breaking point.

I wondered dully whether the other was blaming himself for not having seen through the enemy's plan a little earlier. Dimly, I appreciated that I was almost at the limit of my strength, that exhaustion was pulling at my body with clutching fingers. There was an aching, muzzy feeling behind my forehead so that I could no longer think clearly. All I wanted to do was to lie down somewhere and surrender myself completely to the fatigue in my body.

Jensen thrust open the door of the billet, walked inside. I followed close on his heels. Pausing only to pull off my thick flying jacket and slip off my boots, I threw myself down on the bunk and pulled the blankets over my exhausted body. Someone was moving around in the darkness, but although I turned my head, I could not see them. There was the sound of crockery being clinked together and a moment later, the ground crew sergeant came over to me, a dark, dimly-seen shape, holding something in his hand.

"Better take this before you go to sleep, sir," he said huskily. "It'll put some warmth back into your bones. It must be below freezing out there."

With an effort, I lifted myself up onto my elbows, then swung my legs to the floor. The mug of hot cocoa was scaldingly hot, almost burning my fingers in spite of the numbness in them. I sipped it slowly, feeling the warmth spreading itself through my chilled limbs and stomach.

"How's that, sir?"

I smiled wanly in the darkness. "That's the best mug of cocoa I've ever tasted, sergeant," I said thickly, and meant every word of it.

"I thought I'd better keep some brewing for you, sir, for when you finally got back. How was it this time?"

"Pretty rough," I said slowly. "They had a fighter escort

with them. The first time we've ever known it and we weren't ready for them. We destroyed over half a dozen of their planes and lost three of ours, but one of our pilots is evidently safe. At least, Rundstein saw him bale out and he should have landed safely."

I drained the mug and handed it back to him. He took it and stood looking down at me for a moment, then he turned slowly on his heel and walked away.

"Goodnight, sir," he called over his shoulder. A moment later, I heard the door of the billet open for a moment, felt the swirling draught of bitterly cold air on my legs, then it closed again and there was only the sound of his footsteps fading into the distance.

CHAPTER XV

Interrogation

February. March. April.

The hard winter turned into spring again. The days grew progressively longer, the nights shorter and the enemy bombers began to come over in daylight, attacking with or without fighter cover. The ground fighting had settled down to a steady withdrawal on the Western Front, but in the east, the Russian armies were surging forward in full flood and it seemed that nothing could stop them.

At times, I marvelled at how we managed to remain alive. Daily, we flew missions to the west of Berlin whenever enemy aircraft were reported heading that way, patrolling the air lanes used by the enemy. And then there were the nights. These were, perhaps, the worst of all. Darkness lasted for perhaps six hours and in that time, we went through a period of straining eyes, rising tension and utter weariness which grew steadily worse as the weeks passed.

One by one, the original members of the squadron went out and never came back. Finally, at the end of April, there were only Jensen and myself left. All the rest were new pilots who had joined the squadron since we had been stationed near Berlin. Any hopes that we could ever prevent the enemy from bombing any target they wished, were falling fast.

On the last night in April, I flew my last mission. The sun had just set below the western horizon and although it was so late in the year, there was still a frosty nip in the air and the meteorological experts had promised a fine, clear night which meant that, inevitably, the enemy bombers would put in another appearance.

We climbed slowly to three thousand feet and turned—heading north-west towards the last rays of the setting sun. Half an hour later, we spotted the tight formation of enemy planes as they flew steadily eastwards two or three thousand feet below us. This time, they were alone; there were no fighters with them.

The ground came nearer as we went into a shallow dive, lining ourselves up on the sprinkling of black dots as they began to take evasive action. For a long moment, I seemed to be staring through them. The background of fields and hedges seemed to swell up, to gain an unnatural prominence while the enemy formation which was my principal target, swam away behind a faint blurring of tears.

Savagely, cursing myself for my stupidity, I tore my gaze away from the scene, rested my eyes by looking in another direction, blinking them several times in rapid succession. Almost, I had fallen into the trap which was ever present for the forgetful and the unwary; I had committed one of the cardinal sins of a fighter pilot, staring at the same position for so long that my gaze had become fixed upon it hypnotically, resulting in a lack of detail. Sharply, I turned my head, picked up the enemy formation again, and banked steeply.

The enemy planes were now scattered in all directions, apparently at random, broken out from their original tight cluster which would have made things far too simple for fighter aircraft attacking from dead astern as we were. We would now be forced to aim for individual targets.

I felt a grim smile touch my lips and my face tightened of its own volition. The enemy were scattered, but not too scattered—close enough together to derive a certain mutual benefit from the concentrated barrage which they were capable of putting up once we attacked.

I twisted round. There was no mistaking them now, I thought fiercely. Sunlight glittered off their smooth metal sides—they were our old enemies, the Lancasters again.

Almost directly ahead now, massive wing-tips dipping slightly, the big four-engined bombers banked slowly, ponderously, to port, then straightened onto a course which would take them slightly away from us but still in the direction of Berlin which was their eventual target. And they were climbing, steadily climbing.

Two things were suddenly very clear to me as I gave the engine full throttle and dived down out of the twilit sky. The enemy obviously knew we were there and possibly how pitifully few our numbers really were. They hadn't panicked when they had taken their evasive action. Further, they would know from past experience that they had nothing to fear from the defences on the ground so long as we were in the vicinity, and the pilots could concentrate fully on keeping to their original course, while the gunners concentrated on us.

For fifteen, twenty seconds—it seemed ten times as long as that while I sat there, impatient in my seat—the distance closed. If only I didn't feel so unutterably tired. Where there should have been the stirring exultation of the surging battle thrill, there was nothing but a vague, overall emptiness in my mind. My nerves were all keyed up, it was true, but it was a different kind of tension to that which I had experienced in the good old days.

Then we had been men addicted to the task of total destruction; now we were war-weary men unable to think straight, scarcely able to plan ahead, performing every action mechanically, without thought.

It was now almost dusk. Against the faint ruddy glow in the west, I saw one of the dark shapes move across the sights. A sitting duck!

I fired instinctively. The shuddering racket of the wing cannon hammered at my ears, the vibration tore through the plane in sickening waves; the spitting lines of red and white tracer, flickering blobs of light against the darkening sky, reached out and plucked viciously at the wing of the bomber.

The return fire was immediate. For five, ten seconds, the rear gunner in the enemy plane fired a prolonged, savage burst that licked out towards me. Then the Lancaster slid away, smoke trailing from the starboard inner engine and the converging lines of tracer from my guns, still hammering spitefully, tore along the fuselage and into the rear gun turret.

The enemy's last burst, fired possibly in the split second that he died, struck home. I felt the Messerschmitt lurch drunkenly as the canopy in front of me suddenly radiated a splintering of light across the cockpit as the bullets pierced it. Only vaguely was I aware of the pain in my shoulder.

Instinctively, as the bullets had smashed their way through the transparent plastic, I had glanced down. There was a wide, bloody stain on my flying tunic, spreading slowly, but scarcely any pain; only a feeling of terrible numbness that spread rapidly until my left arm hung limp and useless by my side.

For a moment, my mind seemed stunned, refused to take in the fact that I had been wounded; or the more important, more urgent realisation that the plane was falling swiftly, temporarily out of control. Sharply, I pulled myself together, tightened my grip on the smooth metal of the column with my right hand, and brought the plane back onto an even keel. The altimeter needle was registering less than a thousand feet. I shook my head savagely to clear it. It seemed scarcely credible that I could have dived so far out of control without fully realising it.

Almost before the thought had entered my head, the note of the engine changed abruptly, became more harsh and strident, clamouring savagely, as if something had somehow shaken loose inside. Desperately, I tried to regain height but the plane responded sluggishly and slowly.

I had no other alternative now but to break off the engagement, leave the bombers to the others, and make my way back to Base as best I could. Reluctantly, the Messerschmitt came back onto course.

Down below, something flashed abruptly on the ground at the edge of my vision. Even without a second glance, I knew instinctively, what it was. The stricken Lancaster, plunging earthwards with a speed of close on three hundred miles an hour.

The pain was beginning to make itself felt in my arm and shoulder as I succeeded in turning on course and limped eastwards, seeking the low cloud for cover.

*　　　*　　　*　　　*

There were four men in the room, seated in chairs behind the long table. Outside, there had been an air of feverish, intense activity. Here, there was a quiet, almost studied calm.

"Come inside, Lieutenant," boomed one of the men. He stood up, tall and stocky, his uniform resplendent in gold and the glitter of campaign medals. I felt suddenly shabby beside these men and wondered why the Luftwaffe had insisted on doing me proud like this, why I had been sent from hospital after having my shoulder patched up and told to report immediately to the headquarters in Berlin.

"How's the shoulder, Lieutenant?" asked one of the other men, sitting back in his chair. He eyed me sharply from beneath jet black brows which were drawn together into a straight line of concern.

"The doctor seems to think that it will heal up in a few weeks, sir," I said deferentially.

"Good, good. Sit down, won't you." He indicated a chair in front of the table. "We'd like to ask you a few questions if you don't mind. Nothing really personal, you understand. It was a pity about Jensen being shot down and killed on that last mission of yours. He was a good man. Unfortunately, we don't have many men of his calibre left in the Luftwaffe now."

No, I thought wearily, bitterly. The Luftwaffe will never again be what it was during the early years of the war. All of the glory has died and vanished. The men who built it up into one of the greatest fighting machines of the world had died and their places had been taken by men who knew nothing of what it had stood for, who merely wished to bask in the reflected glory of those who had gone before and had died in the defence of their country.

The third man leaned suddenly across the table, offered me a cigarette, flicked a silver table lighter and lit it for me.

"Thank you, sir."

"Now, we'd like you to give us your report on the work of your squadron since you joined it at the beginning of the war," said the tall man gently. "Take your time and give us as much detail as possible in your own words. In particular, we want to know about the men who served with you. How they reacted at different times. How they died. Everything."

I sat quite still for a long moment at a loss, not knowing what to say. It was a story which was not easy to tell to men such as these, a story of personal things, of men and not of machines. Slowly, I tried to put the story into words, but was consciously aware, all the time, of that fact that it seemed far from plausible, but in spite of that, the four men sat silent and still behind the table, smoking frequently, one or two making brief notes on pads laid out in front of them, but not once interrupting me until I had finished.

Finally, I sat back in my chair, feeling strangely exhausted. There was still a dull, throbbing ache in my shoulder and every tiny movement of my arm sent pain prancing through my body.

"I see. I see." The tall man leaned forward, resting his weight on his elbows, and looked across at me quizzically. "It hasn't been easy for anyone, but you seem to have been hit hard during the past few months. First the battle in the Ardennes where we came so close to defeating the enemy utterly and completely and then your work here, defending Berlin."

"Yes, sir." I stubbed out my cigarette and sat with a sense of uneasiness inside me, waiting for them to go on. The tall man turned to his companions, looked at them for a long moment, then said slowly and quietly:

"Is there anything further you would like to ask, gentlemen?"

There was silence for a long moment, then the man at the far end of the table cleared his throat and said harshly:

"What about the feeling among the new pilots? Do you think they'll live up to the standards of the older men?"

"That's dificult to say, sir," I muttered defensively. Inwardly, I wished that this interview were at an end. These were questions I could not answer fairly and truthfully. Concerning men who were now dead and almost forgotten, I felt myself biased, so that my answers all seemed to be one-sided; and I had the instinctive knowledge that this was not what these men wanted. They were trying to get an all-over opinion, while all I could give them was my own personal account of what I had seen and experienced myself.

In reality, there was little to tell. It did not seem likely that we were to have been singled out from the score of other Luftwaffe units based around the capital. Perhaps, I thought suddenly, they had heard of the near-mutiny at Bitburg and were trying to get details at first-hand, now that almost all of the men concerned in it, were dead, and I was the only survivor.

Gradually, I became aware of the fact that the others had risen slowly to their feet, were looking down at me. The tall man said softly:

"We've had a word with your doctors. They agree that you must be relieved of all flying duties as from today. We will endorse that recommendation."

"But, sir—" I protested.

The other held up his hand. He smiled a little tiredly and there was a curious look in his eyes, almost of defeat, I realised.

"I don't think this will come as a surprise to you, Lieutenant," he said, his voice low, so that I could scarcely make out the words. "But there will be very little flying after a few days. The Russian spearheads are within sight of Berlin. It is only a matter of time before we are forced to capitulate, or suffer the indignity of fighting in our streets. Yes, it is as bad as that, I'm afraid."

"But the Feuhrer, sir?"

"Perhaps he doesn't realise it, maybe he doesn't want to believe it, but we who are in constant touch with things at the front can see the writing on the wall." I sat there for a long moment, listening to the calm, quiet, unhurried voice speaking the words of defeat, and I felt once again, the terrible bitterness sweeping over me. There was a sudden chill in my body and I sucked in a deep breath as I pushed myself up to my feet.

"I think I understand, sir," I said haltingly. "I hope the information I was able to give you was of help."

The others nodded their heads slowly, but it was the man at the far end of the table who spoke first. "We're extremely grateful to you Lieutenant for coming here and answering our questions. Sometimes, we may not get out of touch with the men who are out here doing the actual fighting. I think it is a good thing that we should get these details into perspective once in a while."

"You'll go on leave immediately, of course," said one of the others. I saw him glance down at my shoulder. "Rest is all you need now, and plenty of it. There won't be much more fighting in Germany. Don't tell that to anyone, of course, but there are still a handful of realists left among us who can see that Germany is fighting a losing war, a lost cause, and that there will be no miracle at the eleventh hour to save us. I can only hope that the will of the people will be as strong and courageous in the dark days which inevitably lie ahead for us as it has been during the past few months when everything has been against us."

The other's smile was friendly, but bleak, and there was the grey look of defeat on his bluff features. For a moment, he stood in silence, then gave a brief, almost helpless nod as I shuffled my feet uncomfortably on the floor.

"Where do you intend to go first?" he asked conversationally.

"I'm not really sure, sir," I said slowly. "I think I'd like to meet Jensen's widow if that's at all possible."

"Do you know where she lives?"

"He mentioned Hamburg, sir. But somehow, I don't even know whether she's still alive. I think she'd like to hear from me how he died."

The other smiled gently, then gave a sharp call on the buzzer on the desk. The door behind me opened and a sentry stood there; and I noticed that he still had his rifle slung over his shoulder.

The interview was over, I realised. I shook hands with each of the officers, then walked swiftly towards the door.

Outside, there was warm sunlight in the streets of Berlin, throwing long shadows over the pavements. In the distance, sounding oddly out of place, was a continuous, almost thunderous roar. The war guns of the Russian armies, moving in towards the outskirts of Berlin.

THE END